C.O.P.

THE COLOR OF POWER

C.O.P.
THE COLOR OF POWER

The Odyssey of a Black Cop

SYLVESTER STONE

C.O.P. THE COLOR OF POWER
THE ODYSSEY OF A BLACK COP

iUniverse books may be ordered through booksellers or by contacting:

iUniverse
1663 Liberty Drive
Bloomington, IN 47403
www.iuniverse.com
844-349-9409

ISBN: 978-1-6632-1831-5 (sc)
ISBN: 978-1-6632-2332-6 (e)

Library of Congress Control Number: 2021910074

Print information available on the last page.

iUniverse rev. date: 06/21/2021

CONTENTS

INTRODUCTION

The stories in this book are based in part on actual events. Any characterizations of persons, places, or things are the opinions of the authors. This book is a fictionalized story, which could have taken place at "anywhere" United States. The stories are based on the compilation of several African-American police officers throughout America.

The Color of Power takes place over four decades, from the 1960s to 2020, in the western portion of the United States. The storyline depicts the primary character, Ty (Tyrone Washington), and his journey to become a police officer in America. The trials and tribulations of this journey are complex, intense, and rewarding. The true tribulation is that Ty is Black, and that fact adds an extra layer of complexity to his journey.

The 1960s, '70s, and '80s were turbulent and revolutionary times, as evident by events like the protests in Selma, Detroit, Los Angeles, Baltimore, and many other American cities. The assassinations of Dr. Martin Luther King Jr.; President Kennedy; and his brother, attorney general Robert Kennedy, sent America into a social civil war. These historically significant events had a direct influence on the book's leading character, Tyrone. Career desires flashed through his mind, and until he focused on his final choices—first a police officer and then an army soldier, lawyer, or maybe college professor—these were lofty dreams for any young person in America, especially for an African American.

This story may stir emotions regarding the social and political phenomenon known in America as racism; yes, this social disease still exists in the twenty-first century. *The Color of Power* will provide all readers with social insight, relief, and a better understanding of the symbolism of power and race in America. Enjoy Tyrone Washington's American journey to success and the rich lessons illustrated throughout his travels.

CHAPTER 1

The Racial Revolution— Sixties and Seventies

Why the hell would a young Black kid want to be a cop? History hasn't been kind to Blacks in career success and life in general, especially from slavery to Jim Crow and to affirmative action. Tyrone Washington spent many hours thinking about this question. He also thought about other careers coveted by White America like being a doctor, lawyer, or college professor. The answer was always the same—cop first, military second.

Ty was a different sort of young Black kid in the '70s. He was career-minded at thirteen years old, while his Black and Hispanic friends were smoking marijuana, drinking wine, or gangbanging. Surviving and staying alive were the main goals of most Blacks growing up during the '70s and '80s. The causes of death varied during this period, but the greatest causes appeared to be drugs, gangs, and the police; and many estimated the life expectancy of Black males to range from eighteen to twenty-two years old.

Ty's family life was important. His dad worked hard to take care of the family, while his mother stayed at home and cared for Ty and his siblings. Ty was the middle child; Sandra and Jennifer were the oldest. Norris, Ronald, George, and Samantha were the younger ones. His brothers were very athletic and played sports throughout their lives. Ronald excelled in basketball and track; Norris in baseball; Ty in football. Sandra and Jennifer moved away while Ty was young, and he didn't know his older sisters.

Ty was deeply patriotic and deeply embraced the philosophy of a democratic society represented by the United States of America. In 1974, he began his career quest, his journey to become a cop by talking with family and friends. He faced criticism from other Blacks, who felt he was a sellout, and disdain from Whites, who openly expressed opposition to his goal of being a Black cop.

Ty had just finished some street basketball at the local park when he and some friends had that conversation. "Hey, Ty," asked one friend. "What the hell is wrong with you? The police harass, shoot, and kill us Black folks and treat us like dirt. You would think slavery never ended by the way they talk and treat us. The pooleece are the natural enemy of Black folk, and they symbolize the occupying force of the White status quo."

"Maybe I am the one to change the distrust and unite the police and community," Ty said.

"Really, Ty, how are you going to change Metropolitan PD, the most notorious gang in the country?"

"By joining this gang, maybe I can influence and change the traditional way cops are viewed in the Black community. After all, this is the 70's, 1974 is a good year a new century for America, and maybe I can help keep hope alive, as Dr. King used to say."

Those feelings and beliefs of extreme distrust toward the police by communities of color, especially the Black and Hispanic communities, had spread from Detroit to Newark, to the inner city, and to many cities in the country. The constant use of excessive force, racial oral harassment, and outright racial acts of violence against Blacks were the norm. The news reported daily incidents of White police officers shooting unarmed Blacks nationwide. There were no research studies in the '70s and '80s, but life was dangerous for a young Black male. Ty was going to be the "Black avenger," change the course of police distrust, and help restore trust in communities of color toward the police.

Ty enjoyed watching his favorite TV shows and saw the influence of TV on young people of the day. Some of his favorites were cop shows—*Adam-12*, *Dragnet*, *CHiPs*, and *Starsky & Hutch*. These shows influenced Ty's desire to become a cop, but as he watched them, he didn't see a Black police officer on most of the shows and wondered why.

Ty's family moved from the inner city (ghetto) to the suburbs. The area was much safer and didn't have the frequency of gangs, drugs, and violent crime. The schools in this new suburb were better resourced, the community was safer, and job opportunities were better for his parents. Ty grew up with a new and different perspective on life, and he engaged in various activities to build his stability and path to success.

His mom talked with him about the new area and the many opportunities.

"No worries, Mom. I understand from talking to some friends from the inner city about the danger of drugs, gangs, and crime. I want to play sports and will keep myself healthy and clean."

Tyrone matured and was a natural athlete. At six three and 210 pounds, he thought about a career in the National Football League (NFL), as did many of his high school classmates—many of whom became professional athletes. Ty remained focused on becoming a police officer and/or joining the army.

The suburb gang activity was present but not nearly as violent as in his old neighborhood. Ty became an associate member of a local gang for protection and a status symbol, and he was able to avoid a criminal record. The local gangs weren't as dangerous or evolved, but the threat was there. The new neighborhood consisted of some Black and Hispanic families but mostly Whites. Over time, Ty watched many of them move away from his neighborhood to across-town locations.

The local news always broadcast coverage about highly and politically charged social issues. One of the most controversial issues was the Vietnam War. Many of Ty's friends were drafted and sent to Vietnam. Some never returned.

War—the age-old battle for power, he thought. *Wow, we still haven't figured out how to coexist peacefully in the twentieth century.*

He didn't believe in the concept of war. It seemed illogical for mankind to kill each other in massive numbers for political and ideological reasons. Despite his conflicting ideology, Ty decided to join the army.

He visited a friend, Johnny, and they talked about career opportunities.

"I need to figure out in my mind why I want to join the army as an important step to becoming a cop," Ty said.

"I agree with you, brutha. It doesn't make sense that we as Black men would want to be a part of the White power war machine, the military. Look at the war protests and all the military and the war protests and riots."

"Well, the time is coming. We finish high school soon and will need to make some important life decisions, and right now, I am leaning on joining the army in order to become a cop." Ty was determined.

Ty disparately sought information about why the riots and protests were so violent and appeared in the news every week. Were the protests a result of the ideology, dissatisfaction with our government, or social rebellion? He talked with friends and teachers, and listened to the news.

He watched TV news and saw the disrespect given to American soldiers as they returned from Vietnam. The depth of negativity toward the military and the hateful words used against American soldiers were incorrigible and unpatriotic. Soldiers received malicious and hurtful names like "baby killers," "murdering devils," "rapists," and many other derogatory names. For the most part, these young— seventeen-, eighteen-, or nineteen-year-old—soldiers were boys who couldn't even vote or buy alcoholic beverages. Many had been drafted and served their country, but they were treated so very badly. Ty didn't understand and wondered whether his career choices were honorable.

"Hey, Mom, you know I want to join the army," Ty said to his mom. "But I am curious. Why are so many Blacks sent to Vietnam? I have heard many stories at school and in the park about how White America is sending as many Blacks as possible to Vietnam in hopes that they will be killed and decrease the population of Blacks in America. That is scary. Is it true?"

"Son, our nation calls upon young men to go to war and drafts them into the military. I have heard the same stories, and I believe there is some truth to them. Hopefully, I will not have to find out through you, my son."

Like most Black youth of the time, Ty was faced with black identity philosophies (BIP). The Black philosophies were the Black Panther Party, Black Muslims, and Dr. Martin Luther King Jr's nonviolent approach. He spent years learning about all three philosophies and their distinctive, conceptual traits. Ty talked to his close friend, Lew.

"Hey, man, who is your role model or hero—Malcom, Dr. King, or Eldridge Cleaver (Black Panther Leader)?"

"You know, all have different attributes—the radical Panthers, nonviolent Dr. King, and the religious radical Malcom X." Ty looked deeply into the philosophies.

The Black Panthers were a radical Black militant group founded in October 1966 in Oakland, California, by Bobby Seale and Huey P. Newton. Additional leaders of the party emerged, most notably Fred Hampton and Eldridge Cleaver. The Black Panthers advocated power through force and armed resistance in response to the White American power structure, generally symbolized by the police. The Panthers held rallies and protests to advocate the overthrow of the racist White American government. There were many violent encounters between the police and the Panthers in several cities—San Francisco, Oakland, Detroit, and Chicago, to name a few.

The Black Panthers adopted the "clenched right-handed fist in the air" sign, symbolizing Black power. The fist received international attention during the 1968 Olympics in Mexico City, when the two American sprinters, John Carlos and Tommie Smith, raised their clenched fists in protest of the racial inequalities in America while standing on the winners' podium. Ty remembered sitting in his living room and watching these Olympians raise their clenched fists in protest of the racial inequalities by the American government against Blacks in America.

The primary symbols of the inequality were police harassment and the shooting of Black males. Later in life, Ty was blessed to meet John Carlos, a true American hero. John happened to live in the same neighborhood as Ty. They had frequent conversations regarding racism in America and how unjust the system toward Blacks in America was.

The Panthers based their beliefs to some extent on Mao Zedong's interpretation of the little red book (also called "Mao's Little Red Book"), the *Communist Manifesto* by Karl Marx and Friedrich Engels, which promoted China's version of communism. This presented a problem and conflict for the patriotic Tyrone. He then reviewed the philosophies of the Black Muslims, since the Black Panthers were involved in several shootouts with the police from San Francisco to the inner city.

Next in the philosophies scheme were the Black Muslims, who incorporated and adopted the Islamic religion, believing it was the true religion of American Blacks. Elijah Muhammad (born Elijah Robert Poole) was the leader of the Black Muslims during the '60s and '70s with a theme of "Pan-Africanism," or the Back-to-Africa movement. Muslims believed the White man was the enemy of all people of color and had to be dealt with directly "by any means necessary." Elijah Muhammad was succeeded by Louis Farrakhan. Malcolm X (born Malcom Little) was a top assistant of Muhammad, as was Louis Farrakhan.

The movement was slowed when Malcolm X was killed in 1965, but the Black Muslim faith continued to flourish. After a few years of uncertainty, a new leader emerged, Louis Farrakhan (born Louis Eugene Walcott). The Islamic religion believed in the prophet Muhammad and practiced this faith. Islam was a completely different religion than the traditional Western Judeo-Christian religious beliefs of most American Blacks.

The third philosophy was the nonviolent approach to racial equality advocated by Dr. Martin Luther King Jr., a Baptist minister from Georgia. He was one of the most prominent civil rights leaders during Ty's early childhood. His philosophy was based on the teachings of many Christian writings and the peaceful teachings of Mahatma Gandhi.

Ty spent several years reviewing and analyzing these philosophies. He attended a Black Panther party rally in the neighborhood park with his friend Larry. They arrived at the park and noticed the Panther speaker was a Black US Army Vietnam veteran wearing a blue-jean vest with US Army insignias and emblems. He began describing the Vietnam War.

"I just got back from 'Nam. We don't even belong over there," the speaker said. "Vietnam is the White man's war!

He sends us, the Black man, overseas to a foreign land to fight the Yellow man for democracy, freedom, and justice. But we, as Black people, ain't free in our own country. Look at the job and housing market. We can't even move into nice neighborhoods without the Whites moving out or simply not letting us move in. They find some excuse on the application to disqualify us—our credit, lack of stability, or some other bullshit reason."

"Why did the brothers pick the black panther as their symbol?" Ty asked his friend Larry.

"Because the black panther is a strong and powerful animal. The black panther is one of the few wild animals that cannot be domesticated or kept in captivity. It strikes instant fear into people because of this characteristic and its keen ability to instantly perceive danger and preempt attacks by striking first."

"Wow, what an animal!"

"Brothers and sisters," the speaker continued, "our Black brothers are systematically killed by the White man by sending us to Vietnam. I saw with my own eyes how Black men were always walking point, the first man in a combat patrol. Picture walking down a dirt road and being the first person in line to be shot. Generally the first man in the patrol was carrying the 'pig,' referring to the M-60 machine gun, a heavy weapon with major firepower." The speaker paused. "Listen to me. The point is, the dude with the pig usually gets killed first, and the brothers, us Blacks, were always on point carrying the pig.

"It will be a long time before White America accepts us as equals. Listen to this shit about our American military. During World War II? Black American soldiers weren't allowed to eat in restaurants in the South. Some of you remember the signs on the doors of many places—'Colored People Not Allowed'—or some restaurant signs said, 'Coloreds Enter in the Back Door Only.' Yet German prisoners of war, captured by enemy soldiers, could enter in the front door and were served their meals. Do y'all hear me? Enemy soldiers who killed American soldiers could eat in restaurants because they were White! Yet Black American soldiers were denied this simple privilege!"

The speech ended, and the speaker left the stage and seemingly disappeared into the crowd. Ty ran to catch him. "Sir, I am thinking about joining the army and fighting for democracy."

The vet looked at him and said, "Don't be a fool, young blood! Your country, as you call it, is still fighting the Civil War. Many states in the South still have Civil War statutes memorializing Confederate soldiers! The soldiers of the South were traitors to the United States government and are hailed as historical heroes for many White folk. There will never be peace for a Black man in America until some major changes take place."

"I agree, and I want to be part of the change," Ty replied.

"Spare me your Uncle Tom ideas," the veteran responded in a loud tone, sighing. "Look at all the great Blacks we've had in America—Frederick Douglass, George Washington Carver Marcus Garvey, W. E. B. Du Bois, Sojourner Truth, Dr. Martin Luther King Jr., and many others, including the first man killed in the Revolutionary War, Crispus Attucks. You probably don't even know who I'm talking about. Do you know how many national holidays are dedicated to any Black Americans? Not one!

"I don't want to hear about your desires to be a pig, a police officer. Do you know the White man had to make new laws so Black folks could get equal opportunities in the job market and vote?"

"No shit," Ty said in disbelief.

"The Constitution didn't mean shit!" the vet continued. "This law, the Affirmative Action Bill, was just passed last year. I guarantee it will not last long. Someday some Uncle Tom Black Man will help White people get rid of this law because it benefits and helps Black folks and other minorities in the job market."

The veteran turned and walked away. Ty and Larry left the park.

"Hey, Larry, what do you think?" Ty asked his friend.

"That was some heavy stuff he just laid on us. We are about two years away from becoming eligible for the military draft. Man, no damn way will I go into the military and die for the White man," retorted Larry.

"Really, I think I want to serve the country and change all the crap Blacks have had to put up with over the years," Ty said.

"Brutha, you are crazy! Didn't you listen to what was just said?"

"Yes, but someone has to try to change how White people feel about us, and joining the army is my part."

They walked home from the park and went to their separate homes.

While at home, Ty approached his mom and told her about the speaker and his experiences that day in the park. His mother was a strong, articulate Black woman, who had grown up in the South under the racist Jim Crow segregation laws.

"You see, Son, today as well as when I grew up, racial bigotry and hatred are still very much a part of America. Some say segregation is slavery's little brother because of how it boxed in Black people and limited their development in society. Segregation has denied our people equal education, professional jobs, and good jobs. Jim Crow laws systematically denied Blacks resources, upward mobility, and equal opportunity in the American dream.

"The impact of segregated Black schools resulted in the lack of academic resources, unlike the White schools, who received every resource requested to educate their kids. Therefore, Son, the quality of education needed for success and upward mobility in life wasn't provided to Blacks in the South or anywhere else in America. The one bright star for Blacks in America was the Historically Black Colleges and Universities (HBCUs). They provided the primary higher education for many Blacks in America, who couldn't enroll or be invited to register for the Ivy League colleges. This even meant prestigious state universities."

Ty's mom continued. "In the traditional K–12 Black schools, many of which were generally located in the South, they possess lesser quality of academic resources to include outdated textbooks. Many of the classrooms were substandard with old and broken furniture and classroom equipment. Many of the buildings were very old and filled with mold, mildew, and asbestos.

"Some Whites believed if they could keep Blacks away from education resources, they wouldn't get the tools for success, and thus 'White privilege' would continue and thus be the power base of America. So, when the schools started becoming integrated, the previously denied opportunities for equal access slowly decreased, and education became easier for Blacks. However, the by-product of this created a new era of racial bias and discrimination.

"Son, I think, therefore, blacks scored so low in scholastic aptitude test scores and other academic aptitude exams. If not for Historically Black Colleges and Universities (HBCUs), Blacks wouldn't have achieved success, economic stability, or higher education in meaningful numbers. Son, as you know, Black folks have trouble passing the federal civil service exams, and I think it's because of the segregated schools over the last twenty years.

"Another problem I see emerging today is Black-on-Black crime, and we do not help each other like other minority groups. Asians band together to develop business ventures like the Vietnamese and Koreans. Many of our people don't realize that if we fight and kill each other, we're not a threat to the White majority. Black folk are like crabs in a barrel—when one tries to crawl out, another pulls them back down. If this Black-on-Black crime continues and Blacks continue to participate in gangs, drugs, and criminal activity, the happier Whites will be because we're not a threat to their stability."

"I see, Mom, and I bet someday White bureaucrats will use the Black-on-Black crimes against us when it comes to Black success and allegations of racism. Mom, when will we ever be treated as equals and be allowed into the professions we desire as well?" Ty asked his mom.

"Education is the key, and you must get it!" said his mom. "In this country, Blacks haven't traditionally had the resources to attain success since segregation has seen to that."

"Thanks, Mom! I want to learn as much as I can."

"Son, remember, the ticket to success is education, and I warn you—do not let the hatred of racial prejudice blind you to success. All I have told you is to enlighten you about the world you live in, and I want you to be successful. White people will stick together and pretend to be your friend. Be careful, walk softly, and carry a big notebook. Keep your eyes open and your mouth shut."

"I will, Mom, thanks."

The Black philosophies deeply concerned Ty. Which would he adopt? Which ideology was the most advantageous to him to help him achieve his dream of becoming a police officer? Ty picked the nonviolent approach of the Nobel Peace Prize laureate Dr. Martin Luther King Jr.

Dr. King's belief in human rights, freedom, and true justice for all oppressed people impressed Ty, who had spent hours listening to Dr. King's radio messages and watching him on TV. Dr. King's messages of peace, justice, and honor to all was his philosophical view; he believed in achieving justice through nonviolent means. Dr. King had staged nonviolent protests in cities across America with other Black civil rights leaders like the Reverend Jesse Jackson, Ralph Abernathy, Andrew Young, and a young John Lewis.

Even though his method was nonviolent, Dr. King was arrested for protesting and was brutally treated and beaten as though he were a criminal. Ty wondered why this great man of peace had been hunted and hounded like an animal. Why did so many Whites, especially the police, degrade and demonize the nonviolent civil rights movement? Dr.

King was a man who exemplified peace and promoted the harmonious coexistence of all mankind; his ill treatment was simply wrong and un-American.

Violence met Dr. King on April 4, 1968, in Memphis, Tennessee. Ty remembered hearing the news bulletin. "Dr. Martin Luther King Jr. has just been shot. Stand by for details." Within a few minutes, the news of his death filled the airwaves. The world and all mankind had lost a true American hero.

His legacy lived on in the minds of many people around the world, and Dr. King was a great role model for Tyrone Washington.

During all this thinking, there was high school. Ty and Johnny walked to school and discussed all kinds of stuff; the death of Dr. King was one of them. As an African American, Johnny believed Dr. King's philosophy was the best approach for America. He didn't believe the Black Panthers or Black Muslims were the right approaches because White America demonstrated a misunderstanding of these philosophies. In other words, although there were some positives to the Muslims and Panthers, White America would dig in and oppose anyone who advocated these viewpoints. After school, Ty, Johnny, and Larry went to football practice and forgot about national events. After practice, they were joined by two other friends, Michael and William. These young Black males went to the local shopping center and sat around at the doughnut shop, eating doughnuts and talking about their future as Black males in America.

"You know, as a Black man, I am worried about making it to twenty-one years of age. The statistics clearly show

Blacks are 99% more likely to be drafted and sent to Vietnam to die," said Michael.

"Yeah, maybe killed by the police," William added. "We should be the ones to change our destiny. Maybe Whites will give us fair chances to succeed in our future."

"We are learning in school the promise of fairness and equal treatment to everyone regardless of color," Johnny said. "If we study hard and stay out of trouble, maybe we can be the generation to change White America. What do you think, Ty?"

"I agree with everything you guys are saying. My contribution for the change is to become a police officer."

"You have talked about being a cop for years," Johnny said. "Remember, even though we want fair treatment and follow the rules, other young Blacks do not. Guess what? You will have to face them!"

"Right on!" William replied. "We must move forward and at least do our part through individuality and apply what we are learning in school. Brothers, we graduate from high school next year. What will it be? College? Military?"

They all left the park, went home, and continued having these conversations.

The following year arrived, and in 1975 at eighteen years old, Ty graduated from high school, was eligible for the military draft and faced the reality of Vietnam. While waiting to be drafted or deciding to enlist, Ty enrolled in junior college. During his first semester, Johnny, Willie, and William called him and told him they had received drafts notices and had been inducted into the army. Ty continued his college education and enjoyed two years of college life, including the joys of playing football.

Ty's college major was criminal justice. He hoped this college major would enable him to become a police officer. There were many discussions about becoming a cop in these classes. However, something was missing. They sat in the college cafeteria one afternoon and talked about policing.

"So, Tyrone," asked Pablo, a classmate, "why do you want to be a cop? Most Black people are committing crimes and being arrested."

"I want to make a difference and show all you White people that Blacks can be productive and positive contributors in American society."

"Well, good luck with that," another White classmate said. "You realize that, even though you are in college trying to better yourself, White people will suspect your motives in wanting to become a police officer."

"I'm not sure what you mean, but okay, I will set a new trend." Ty left the cafeteria and drove home.

Wow, this is going to be challenging and harder than I believed, Ty thought. *Oh well. I will stay the course.*

During his community college days, Ty started taking written civil service examinations to become a police officer. He failed most of the written exams and didn't know why. After several attempts, a frustrated and defeated Ty asked his mom for advice.

"Mom, I failed another exam. I don't understand. I am a junior college student and still cannot pass a written exam."

"Son, going to college is a good choice," his mother said. "Remember, you are a Black man, and it is 1974! Great strides may have been made but look around. How many Black police officers have you seen?"

He remained silent.

"The exam is not tailored for minorities," his mother added. "In other words, the exam is biased against minorities. Take a break from trying so hard and try another path to your dream."

"Thanks, Mom, I will do some soul-searching," Ty finally replied. "Maybe joining the army would be good!"

Ty was becoming very frustrated, and his mind wandered. Was he the only Black applicant? Why was he failing? Was his mom right? Were the philosophies of the Black Panthers or Malcom X a better choice? Maybe the nonviolent movement of Dr. King was better with key events like the Selma-to-Montgomery marches? Had Bloody Sunday in 1965 been worth the pain and suffering of the participants? Had Dr. King been assassinated in vain?

Yes! thought Ty. All these questions clouded his vision, but how would he move forward?

CHAPTER 2

Molded by the Military

As a community college student, Ty began the first step in his quest to become a police officer by taking written civil service examinations. He failed several of the exams, yet he pressed forward and continued taking the examinations. He asked a fellow classmate, Sam, a police officer, for advice on passing the written exam.

"You have to focus on your writing and reading comprehension skills. I failed several of my first few written exams. Hang in there and never give up."

"Sam, getting past this first step is such a burden," Ty said. "Others seem to breeze past the exam, but it is so hard for me, and I know in order to get hired, I must get pass this first step."

"That is true, Ty, true, but others have problems passing the exam as well."

"What puzzles me the most is that I know some of our classmates have not only passed the written but moved on in the hiring process and were hired as police cadets or trainees but not me! I know for a fact many of them have smoked dope, been arrested, and have minor criminal records. I have no criminal record and have never been in trouble."

"Ty, stop complaining. Pass the written exam, and then we will discuss getting hired. I know it is a pain in the ass. However, the process doesn't get any easier."

"I think there is a racial component in the hiring process of police officers. I am concerned about it. I heard from many friends how hard it is for the average Black applicant."

"We are getting better in America," Sam said. "I hate to say this, but as a White guy, racial prejudice still exists, even in the 1970s. I have listened to other White officers making racial slurs and jokes. I admit it is easier for me than you, even after the difficulty of the written exam. I was hired as a police cadet and shortly thereafter a police officer. You know, Ty, maybe you should join the army and get some additional life experience in a structured training environment."

"Sam, that is bullshit," Ty protested. "I am a twenty-year-old Black American male with no criminal record, and there is no reason I should not be hired, and running away to the army should not be the solution."

"I understand that may not be your first choice, but it is an option to buy valuable time in working through the process to get hired. Ty, don't be naïve. Of course you should not have to join the army to prove worthiness or gain life experience. Remember what I told you earlier. Racial prejudice still exists in policing today, and the army may provide you with the tolerance and tenacity to deal with the racial injustices we still experience in America today."

"Thanks, Sam, I will look into the military option and discuss it with my parents."

Ty's frustration and stress continued to build; even after passing the written exam, he was rejected for hire. The reasons weren't explained. The agencies just said he didn't score high enough to be hired. During this examination process, Ty worked hard in college and decided to finish his education and then join the army. He graduated from college with an associate of arts degree in criminal justice and joined the army.

One day Ty sat with his mom and dad after a great dinner of fried chicken and mashed potatoes, and talked to them about joining the military.

"Son," his mother began, "the military is a good choice because I don't think America is ready for Black police officers. Have you noticed how few of those you ever see here in the city?"

"Mom, I have only seen one, and that was only one time."

"Son, here are some lessons to remember. Values are learned as we mature. The racial upheaval in America during the sixties and seventies was challenging to every young American, specifically to young Black Americans. Watch your tongue, and despite how you feel, respect the police, even when you are mistreated. They have the power of life and death, more so with Blacks. Finally, don't make smart-ass comments or challenge their authority!"

"Do not be fooled—the military is a challenge, and racism exists there as well," his dad said. "I think the impact of racism is minimized in the military because there are Blacks at all levels in the military, unlike in policing. If this is your choice, you must be the best soldier. Learn to listen, work hard, and follow orders. At the end of your army tour, you will be more responsible, disciplined, and ready to become a police officer."

"Thanks, Mom and Dad. I will do my best to serve this country."

The next day, Ty walked into the army recruiter's office and discussed an army future and enlistment options. After a couple of weeks of negotiating options with the recruiter and sharing with friends, he joined the US Army. He was offered several different military occupation specialties (MOS), including the military police (MP), infantry, artillery, and communications. Ty selected the military police MOS.

He spent the next few weeks preparing to leave home for the first time to attend basic military training. His friends held a small going-away party for him at the home of Larry, where the only foods consumed were sodas, water, and cookies. The friends exchanged lies of heroism and conquering, as only young men could do.

His parents drove him to the bus station for the long trip to basic training at Fort Ord, California, located on the beautiful Monterey Peninsula. He hugged and kissed his parents, boarded the bus, and was joined by his friend Reggie. To pass the time, Reggie, Ty, and the other recruits shared stories or exchanged lies of conquest, as only young males can do.

"So what do you guys think the training is going to be like?" Ty asked.

"I heard they shoot at you while you're running with full combat gear on," one guy said.

"Yeah, and I heard the drill sergeants beat you up whenever they want."

The stories became boring, and one by one, the recruits fell asleep. Ten hours later, they arrived at the army reception center in front of a huge sign that said, "Welcome to Fort Ord, California." The recruits were all sleeping, and when they arrived, it was about midnight.

Suddenly, the ground around the bus started shaking, and the air was filled with the thundering sound of men shouting at them.

"Wake up, you maggots, get your sleepy asses out of this bus!"

These men were dressed in green army fatigue uniforms, wearing dark-green wide-brim hats. The drill sergeants had arrived.

"This ain't Hollywood or Disneyland. Get your asses in line!"

The recruits lined up as best they could. The drill sergeants circled them and continued yelling at the new recruits. "All right, shitheads, let's see if you all can count and walk at the same time! Forward … march! One, two, three, four. Left, right, left, right!"

The disoriented recruits did their best to march, and after a few feet, they stopped in front of a large building—the barracks.

The drill sergeants, clearly identified by their coveted "Smokey the Bear" hats, said to the recruits, "Get a good night's sleep, ladies, because tomorrow will be a day you will never forget."

The drill sergeants left the barracks, but all of them stayed awake for a while and discussed their first day in the army—in other words, they talked shit.

"That wasn't so bad," one recruit said.

"Don't be stupid," Ty said. "Tonight was a walk in the park. I bet tomorrow will be hell on earth. We'd better get some sleep. Those drill sergeants will be knee-deep in our asses tomorrow."

"Yeah, Ty, you are probably right."

Someone turned out the barracks light, and they settled down and went to sleep.

The next day lived up to everyone's fears about military training. The thunderous screaming by the drill sergeants started again at four a.m.

"Get the hell out of those bunks, you lazy shits!" a voice barked out.

Everyone was still in bed, and one recruit said, "Hey, man, it's fucking four in the morning. I'm going back to sleep."

A drill sergeant walked over to where the brave fool was in bed and said, "Too early, huh?"

The drill sergeant grabbed the bunk and dumped the mattress on the floor with the recruit still on it. "Now you get your little ass outside and stand in formation."

Needless to say, the recruit and the others ran outside, still in their underwear, and stood in some type of formation. The recruits scrambled back to the barracks, got dressed, and returned to the street in their clothes. A light rain began to fall as the recruits stood in formation.

"You shitheads are going to begin processing into the unit," one drill sergeant said in front of about a hundred guys. "Stay in some sort of order and walk straight."

Then he started counting, "One, two, three four."

The recruits tried to walk in cadence, but it was unsuccessful and looked terrible. They walked to a large warehouse, where the uniforms and field gear were issued, which included ammo belts, ammunition magazines and holders, shovels, backpacks, and sleeping bags. Everything was thrown into a big green sack, better known as a duffel bag. This was exciting for Ty—at last, real army uniforms. Even though he was just a private, he felt a sense of accomplishment.

The recruits placed their uniforms in their duffel bags and were marched to the barracks area by all six drill sergeants, who were yelling and screaming at the recruits, "Your left right, left right, one, two, three, four," as the recruits repeated the drill sergeants in a cadence. Ty was assigned to A Company, Second Battalion, Third Training Brigade, at Fort Ord, California. The recruits of A Company returned to the barracks area with two duffel bags full of clothes and equipment. They remained in the street outside the barracks, where the formation was to be held regularly.

Drill Sergeant Shorty stood out front and yelled, "Okay, you maggots! On my command, fall out of this formation and go get dressed in your new uniforms. You have five minutes! Fall out!"

The recruits hurried inside the barracks, the Drill Sergeant yelled, "assholes and elbows" hurry up! They tossed their duffel bags on the beds and returned half-dressed to the formation, scared to be late. The recruits were now in their new, non-ironed army uniforms (green fatigues) and stood before the drill sergeants. Then it began.

The drill sergeants went from recruit to recruit, asking each, "Why isn't your uniform starched and pressed? Who the hell shined your boots? Looks like you shined them with a damn Hershey chocolate bar! You damn recruits

25

better have your boots polished and uniforms pressed by tomorrow, or we are going to run your asses up and down these hills all fucking day! Fall out, get out of here, and prepare for barracks inspection."

The recruits raced back inside the barracks and tried to put their gear inside the footlocker in front of each bed and the wall locker next to each bed.

Suddenly, one recruit yelled, "Someone is coming up the stairs."

The terrified recruits stopped putting away their gear and lined up at the position of attention next to their individual bunks. A large man stood in the shadow of the doorway of the barracks, and his figure filled the entire doorway. He began walking in the center of the barracks.

"I am Drill Sergeant Bearcat, your father and mother for the next eight weeks," he shouted. "I must get you shitheads ready for combat. You are the worst-looking bunch of flesh I have ever seen. There is a war going on, and I don't want any of you to get me or any other soldier killed, so you'd better listen and pay attention to every fucking thing I tell you!"

Drill Sergeant Bearcat walked over to one recruit, and suddenly the ground started shaking. A group of four other drill sergeants, "Smokey the Bear" hats and all, entered the barracks and swarmed the shaking recruits.

The first one, Drill Sergeant Shorty, shouted, "Get your asses outside in the street in front of the barracks. Move!"

The recruits ran outside and lined up as best as they could.

"Watch me, maggots," Drill Sergeant Too Tall shouted. "I am going to show you how to do military turning movements. Don't forget and pay attention! This is how you make a right face, left face, and about-face!"

As all this was taking place in their formation, Drill Sergeant Tuna walked around the company, shouting, "Listen, listen, you bunch of sorry-ass recruits!"

In addition, their assigned drill sergeant, Bearcat, along with Drill Sergeant Cool, walked up and down the company line formations, tucking in shirttails and straightening the hats on the recruits.

"What the hell? This was day one in the army?" one recruit said.

This routine lasted about four weeks. By week four, some of the drill sergeants backed off with some of the in-your-face screaming and simply barked commands, and the recruits understood what to do. The new company of recruits was slowly turning into an organized mob of recruits and soon, army basic trainee soldiers.

Ty was selected as the recruit platoon leader, and he was responsible for 28 out of the company's 120 soldiers. This was his first leadership role in life, and he learned quickly to care for others. In basic training, a platoon leader is responsible for managing four subordinate leaders, called "squad leaders," who maintain accountability of the seven soldiers in their squad. This is also how the army goes into battle. Ty worked hard at making sure his platoon performed to the rigid standards of Drill Sergeant Bearcat. Physical training (PT) was a primary emphasis during army basic training, and the training better prepared trainees for the rigors of combat.

Ty's daily routine was listening to the shouting of orders by the drill sergeants and those familiar words. "All right, shitheads, let's go, double time!"

The running began with cadence or singing to keep the recruits in step. The company ran about two to eight miles daily, depending on how the drill sergeants felt that today. One cadence went like this: "Up in the morning with the rising sun, gonna run all day till the running's done, one, two, three, four." The recruits repeated the cadence as they ran up the hills, through the sand, and back onto the hard stand (asphalt-paved barracks area).

Seven miles later, they were back in the company area and in front of the barracks. They were dismissed for that day's training, and the recruits headed to their bunk beds.

Ty and his buddy Hillbilly, located in the bunk next to Ty's, often discussed the training and the significance of the different ribbons and medals worn by the drill sergeants.

"Hey, Ty, did you notice all the drill sergeants have combat infantry badges?" Hillbilly asked.

"What the hell is that?" asked Ty.

"I read in an army manual that the combat infantry badge (CIB) is given to those soldiers who were in combat and assigned to a line infantry unit. I hope I can earn such an honorable award," replied Hillbilly.

"You do know that means going to war and getting directly involved in combat operations, right?"

"Yeah, I know. That's what being in the army is all about—going to war for democracy and the freedoms we all enjoy."

All of them nodded and finished polishing their boots. Then it was lights off—another day done.

Ty thought about the eventuality of one day going to war and being in a combat zone. The prospect was a bit concerning, but he believed in being an American soldier. He switched gears one day when his friend Pedro came by his bunk and started talking about race.

"Hey, Pedro, what do you think about Black power?"

"It's cool," Pedro answered. "We Chicanos are following the lead of our Black brothers and chanting, 'Brown power.' The future looks bright for race relations and equal opportunity. I hope more minorities are promoted to general officer."

"I agree," Ty replied. "So far, I have never seen a Black, Hispanic, or female general officer."

The next day while in formation, a frustrated recruit opened his stupid mouth and challenged a drill sergeant to a fight. "You know, if you didn't outrank me, I'd kick your little ass up and down this pavement. You guys think those Yogi Bear hats make you invincible? They don't. Your ass can be kicked!"

The other recruits were amazed.

"What a dumb shit," one recruit whispered.

"That's enough, Private," the drill sergeant replied. "You will report to KP (kitchen police), peeling potatoes as discipline at 1700 hours."

"I ain't doing shit, and I'm tired of this army bullshit!"

The drill sergeant stepped back. "All right, Private, do you still want to kick my ass?"

"You got that shit right."

"Fine, let's walk behind the barracks."

The drill sergeant was five nine and weighed 160 pounds; the private stood at six four and weighed about 230 pounds. Being a former high school football star didn't matter in the army.

The two squared off, and Private Badass took a swing at the drill sergeant and missed. No one could count how many times the drill sergeant hit Badass as he was falling to the ground. The drill sergeant turned and faced the recruits, who had gathered around to see the spectacle.

"Let this be a lesson to you all! Whether you are a street hoodlum, high school sports star, or an academic genius—you cannot come into the army and run your damn mouth."

The drill sergeant casually walked away, leaving Private Badass on the ground. This display impressed Ty. To him, this incident illustrated army values of honor, stability, and intestinal fortitude to handle problems. Yes, this wasn't in policy or the law, but in the '70s, this was okay.

As the weeks passed, the recruits were becoming soldiers, running in unison, marching in perfect step, and acting as a unit. Eight weeks seemed to fly by, and now graduation was within striking distance. The blood, sweat, and tears of basic training were coming to an end. The rifle ranges, combat patrol training, and hand-to-hand combat training were finally over. Graduation day was upon them. This was a significant event for Ty, because it ushered in his passage to manhood and self-independence.

The big day arrived, and the new army soldiers put on their class-A uniforms, nicely pressed shirt, tie, green pants, and coat. The new recruits had very few awards or medals. Ty's mother attended his graduation ceremony. She sat in the reviewing stands with the other parents and some family members.

"Son, I am very proud of you," Ty's mom said after the ceremony. "This is a milestone and a step toward achieving your lifelong goal of becoming a police officer."

Ty respected and admired his cadre of drill sergeants: Shorty, Cool, Too Tall, and the mighty Bearcat, whom he admired most.

"Thank you, Drill Sergeant, for training me to be a good soldier," Ty said, a little nervous and shaky as he walked up to Drill Sergeant Bearcat. "I will never forget you and my army training."

"No problem, son. That's what I do," Bearcat responded sincerely. "And you will be a good soldier. I can tell."

A surprised and happy Ty popped to attention, saluted Bearcat, and walked away.

The recruits sat in the barracks one last time, waiting for their next assignments.

"Well, guys," Ty said, "I'm headed to military police school. Man, we went through some shit here. Let's stay in touch."

"That's true," Pedro replied. "We did it. Be cool, Tyrone. I'll see you someday."

Pedro was headed to infantry school at Fort Benning, Georgia. None of Ty's basic training friends would be joining him at MP school. They had all gone on to infantry, artillery, and chemical schools. Ty went home for a few days to say goodbye to his brothers and neighborhood friends. He said one last goodbye to his mom and dad. Next stop— advanced individual training (AIT).

After a couple of days of vacation at home, Ty boarded a plane at Inner-City International Airport (LAX), and after four hours, he landed in Atlanta, Georgia. He boarded a bus to Fort Gordon, Georgia, located near the city of Augusta. He recalled some words from his mom. "Georgia is not California, and although it is 1977, do not forget you will be in the South, and it is very culturally different from California. Do not date or look at White girls like you did in California."

Indeed, Georgia was clearly different from the asphalt jungles of the inner city. Ty saw green trees, rolling hills of vegetation, and flowing rivers. This was his first time away from his home state of California and the first time to see green trees and flowing rivers. Ty and a few other soldiers boarded a bus for Fort Gordon, Georgia. Upon arrival, he reported to the MP school headquarters building. After checking in, Ty was assigned to a barracks, where he met other soldiers from across the country. AIT was very different from basic training. Not as many yelling or screaming drill sergeants; the "Smokey the Bear" hats were still in training, but the focus was on training the soldiers.

The army's military police school was a police academy in the military where basic law enforcement training and military combat operations were taught. It was referred to as "military operations in urban terrain" (MOUT). The training consisted of learning how to fire heavy weapons, such as the M2 machine gun, M72 LAW, and the Mk 19 grenade launcher. The army's mission was stressed throughout training. "The job of the army is to win America's wars." The eight weeks of training also included military customs, physical security of special weapons facilities, and road MP duties.

During the first training course, the post commander, Colonel Root, welcomed the trainees. He greeted them to the army's foremost military police training school. Ty's company of about eighty soldiers joined the brigade of about five hundred soldiers in the post theater. After the welcome, the soldiers returned to their individual company areas and began the training day with physical training.

The second week of MP school was the race relations course. Race relations were important to the welfare and general morale of the army; thus, race relations courses were designed for all army soldiers. The soldiers attending came from various ethnicities but were mostly Black and White. The rest of the country was in racial turmoil, with riots and protests erupting from coast to coast. The military recognized the importance of race relations and held these classes for all soldiers' military training.

The responses from some of the White soldiers expressed how important it was to maintain the "White culture" of the South—meaning, maintaining the statutes dedicated to Civil War heroes of the South. The Black soldiers argued the Civil War had been necessary to prevent slavery from spreading throughout America, and no monument or statute representing slavery should be permitted to stand in the United States of America. However, in 1977 the statutes and monuments remained.

The two-day, four-hour course was productive and promoted a positive exchange of feelings and beliefs between White and Black soldiers. During this time, Ty noticed the focus was on White and Black soldiers; however, the number of Hispanic soldiers started increasing, and many shared the same concerns as the Black soldiers.

Later that same week, Ty and some of his barrack buddies decided to see the sights of Augusta, Georgia. The first stop was a local nightclub, where the fellas could get their groove on.

As Ty and his buddies stood in line, the bouncer at the front door walked over to them and said to his buddies, "You guys can go in, but he"—the bouncer pointed at Ty—"can't go inside."

"Why?" asked a soldier.

"Because he is Black, and we don't allow them in our club."

"What the hell is wrong with you?" the soldier Bill responded. "This is America, and we are American soldiers, all of us! If he can't go in, none of us will!"

The angry soldiers walked away from the club and lost their desire for any other visits to this part of Georgia.

This was Ty's first experience with overt racism. He had heard stories of overt racism and discrimination in the South but had never experienced it directly. While returning to the post, Ty was silent; this situation had been traumatic, and his thoughts were everywhere. The impact of this incident would remain with Ty for years. Upon returning, the soldiers sat around the barracks and drank a few beers before going to bed.

Ty and his new friends enjoyed the training at this army MP school. The trainees walked patrol through an abandoned makeshift "Combat Town" with their weapons. There were opposing forces who fired blank ammunition at them to simulate enemy firing at them. The objective of

Ty's unit was to return fire with overwhelming force and seize the town. This training involved classroom tactical scenarios and then practical application through the physical operational training in Combat Town. As a military police unit, this was the essence of the two-month military police school.

One of the differences from basic training was the day room, or social meeting room, which wasn't available to basic training recruits. The day room had pool tables, table tennis, board games like checkers, and a TV. This room provided the soldiers with some sense of relaxation and recreation. During most lunch hours, the trainees relaxed in the day room.

A news bulletin suddenly came on the TV. President Johnson addressed the nation, saying the war in Vietnam was officially over, and finally the soldiers were coming home. It was 1975, and the soldiers in the day room cheered, trainees expressed a big sigh of relief ("We're not going to war!"), and the stress level was down. They finished training and started the completion phase of military police and another military graduation.

Graduation from military police school was another milestone for Ty in his quest to become a police officer. The trainees entered the final week of training, which included rehearsing the graduation march on the parade field. Graduation day arrived, and the trainees who were becoming US Army military police soldiers marched in front of the command staff and family members. Unlike basic training, the new MPs were marched to the company area after the reviewing stand and held in formation. The company commander handed each soldier his certificate or diploma for satisfactory completion of MP school.

The graduation party was held in the evening at the enlisted ranks' club. There were beer, pizza, and stories; future careers were discussed. Finally, the all-night party ended, and the drunk MP soldiers fell asleep. Alcoholic beverages were unfortunately a foundation of military training. Only the strong resisted abusing beer, wine, and hard liquor. Ty was one of those. He drank a couple of beers from time to time, not a six-pack of beer every other day like many of his trainee buddies.

The day after graduation in the barracks, the first sergeant issued the duty assignments. Ty was assigned to the republic of West Germany. He packed his duffel bag, said his goodbyes to his classmates, and headed home to California for a one-week leave (a.k.a. vacation) before flying to Germany.

Ty went home, visited his parents, and spent a few nights with Johnny and a few other friends from high school. The week went by fast, and it was soon time for Ty to fly to Germany. His mom transported him to LAX. At the airport, she kissed him goodbye, and he boarded the 747 to Germany. This was Ty's first cross-Atlantic, international flight; though he was nineteen, crossing the Atlantic Ocean made him nervous. But it was a long flight to Germany, about eleven hours from LAX. He slept most of the flight and watched whatever movie was being shown. The plane landed in Frankfurt, West Germany, at the Rhein-Main Air Base at about four o'clock in the afternoon, local time.

For the first time in his life, Ty was in another country. This kid from the south-central inner city was now in West

Germany. Ty and several other soldiers exited the 747 and boarded waiting buses at Rhein-Main Air Base; they traveled to temporary military housing a few miles away. During the bus ride, he was amazed by how green the countryside looked, with green trees and flowing rivers like Georgia. He saw a German police car, and it was unlike any police car he'd seen. It was a green-and-white Volkswagen bug with "Polizei" on the side of the doors.

The buses arrived at the US Army Reception Center in Frankfurt. A tall sergeant, first class, greeted the bus and ordered the soldiers to fall into formation. The group formed up, and the sergeant began announcing unit assignments: "Jones, Bitburg Air Base; Smith, Weisbaden; Washington, Baumholder." Ty was assigned to the Eighth Infantry Division, Baumholder, West Germany. He and several other soldiers boarded the bus and headed to their new home.

Four hours later, the bus pulled into the gate of the fortified military compound in Baumholder. They were greeted by another sergeant. "All right, newbies, unass this bus and fall into a formation." The soldiers filed out of the bus and got into a formation, where the assignments were given to the soldiers.

"Private Tyrone Washington, you are assigned to Second Battalion, Bravo Company, with a report-in time of 0700 hours. Your sponsor is Corporal Country. He will contact you in the morning here at Brigade HQ barracks."

The next morning, Corporal Country greeted Ty. "Morning. Are you Private Tyrone Washington?"

"Yes, I am."

"Welcome to Germany. Trust you had a good trip from the States?"

"Yes. Long but fine."

As they talked and walked in the company area, Ty noticed a fenced-in security storage area.

"What kind of duty is this?" Ty asked Country as they walked to the barracks room. "I signed up for MP road or patrol duty."

"Suffice it to say, you will not be riding in any military police car wearing that famous white hat or kicking any ass in the local bars," Country said. "We are assigned to the physical security facility to guard American missile silos here in Germany. You're a guard in a tower—a.k.a. a 'tower rat'—making sure no one jumps the fence and steals our nuclear missiles."

They arrived at the facility, and Ty was taken to his barracks room, his home for the next year.

This is some bullshit, Ty thought. *All that training at MP school, and boom, I'm a security guard? Oh well, I'm a soldier, and I will do my best.*

The days were long and consisted of twelve-hour shifts of sitting in a twenty-foot-high tower in a six-by-six-foot room. The tower was surrounded by a ten-foot-high barbed-wire fence. He didn't like the boring duty of sitting in a twenty-foot-high tower and watching the trees and birds every day to protect the missile silos. He made the best of his time in Germany, and he frequently made visits to nearby towns. The closest to him was the city of Koblenz. He visited the city often because of the pretty girls and good food.

Ty appreciated the hospitality of the German people, who were nice to him. Not only was he a good tourist in Germany, but he also visited several European countries during his three-year tour in Germany. His travels were wonderful, but work remained boring and unchallenging. The life of a tower rat wasn't fun and didn't come close to the excitement he had dreamed of as an army MP.

Ty was assigned guard tower duty. It was about ten-by-ten-feet wide, with two six-foot-wide windows, where the guard could see the tree line of the forest. The site was a missile silo, and MPs were used to guard the site. MPs scanned the tree line to ensure no intruders tried to enter the silo. There was one wire phone in the tower used to call the silo office, where the sergeant of the guard and reactionary force were housed. If any of the guard towers saw someone trying to scale the ten-foot, barbed-wire fences, the guard called the reactionary force, and they responded to neutralize the threat.

This sucks. All of that army training, and I am stuck here, looking at those damn trees and watching for the enemy who never comes, Ty thought while sitting in one of the towers. *Man, I start seeing things, and this midnight shift is scary! I have an M16 with several magazines of ammunition and no one to shoot. I'm here playing solitaire, dreaming of stuff to do, and thinking about California.*

After twelve months of what seemed like boring, unproductive duty, Ty paid his dues and was eligible to submit a transfer request to a patrol MP duty. Patrol duty was the exciting part of being an army MP.

At least to pass the boredom, when he wasn't in the towers, he visited the sights of Germany in his VW bug. Not every soldier had a car, and the decision to buy one had made Ty popular with the other soldiers.

Ty had a new experience in Germany at his small missile silo compound; he associated with Black soldiers for the first time. When Ty moved from the inner city to the suburbs, he lost some of his Black friends from LA. Ty enjoyed this new exposure; he was reintroduced to his roots. The Black soldiers seemed to trust each other more and tended to socialize together. Again, this experience was new for Ty, and he embraced it.

The hanging out included visiting tourist sites in the famous German wine and beer cellars, festivals, and nightclubs. Ty dated a couple of different girls in Germany, and he really enjoyed this experience because these pretty ladies—fräuleins—were simply nice; plus, they liked brothers (male Blacks). The association with Black soldiers provided a safe and secure nurturing environment for Ty, and to him the '70s were exciting.

Ty's transfer finally came through, and he was assigned to a white-hat MP unit. The reporting date was in seven days. Ty packed his clothes into his duffel bag and had a couple of last-night sessions with his buddies and his girlfriend in Koblenz. She promised to visit him in Nuremberg.

The seven days went by quickly, and Ty said goodbye to Corporal Country, who had introduced him to Germany. Ty also spent some time with the brothers, who warned him about being too close to other White soldiers.

"Remember, brutha, you are still Black and not privileged. Do not trust anyone White."

"Thanks, brothers, stay in touch," Ty said.

As he exited the barracks, two of the Black soldiers waved the Black power fist at Ty and said, "Stay Black, power to the people."

"Cool. You guys too."

Ty headed south on the autobahn to Nuremberg, which was about a four-hour trip, and he pulled into the gates at his new unit, the 793rd MP Battalion in Nuremberg, West Germany. Ty walked into headquarters and approached the sergeant sitting at the desk.

"Good morning, Sergeant. I'm reporting for duty. Here are my orders."

The clerk, Corporal Dakota, took his orders and showed him to the first sergeant's office.

"Come in, Private First Class," said the first sergeant. "We have been expecting you. Your sponsor is Sergeant Alert. Here are your promotion orders. Congratulations on your transfer and promotion. You will be officially promoted during formation on Tuesday to corporal."

Ty beamed with surprise and satisfaction as he walked outside to meet Sergeant Alert.

"Welcome, Private First Class, or should I say Corporal? You can call me Bill. Only call me Sergeant around the command staff."

"Thank you, Sarge," Ty said.

On their way to the barracks, Ty asked, "What's the duty like here, Sarge?"

"I think you'll like it. There's good MP action here. You will get some 'stick time.'"

Ty had a single room in his MP barracks, a first for him in the army. He called his mom and told her the great news.

"Congrats, Son. Stay the course. You will be home before you know it and can apply your military experience."

What a great day for Ty in the army!

The next morning, Ty reported to formation, along with the other sixty soldiers in the small MP company, quickly noticing most of the MPs were White with a few Blacks, about ten in the unit. As he was learning, Ty associated more with the Black soldiers, but he also became friends with the White MP soldiers.

The captain, the company commander, stood in front of the formation and, along with the first sergeant, announced there were several new soldiers, and they were going to do promotions. Ty was the third name called, and he marched sharply to the front of the formation and faced the captain.

The first sergeant read the order as Captain Rookie pinned on the rank of the newly promoted soldiers. "The following persons are promoted as follows: Privates First Class Gonzales, Fields, and Washington. You are all hereby promoted to the rank of corporal, United States Army."

What a way to start a new tour of duty!

Formation concluded, and Ty was assigned to his training officer, Corporal Montana, a White guy from New Jersey. This was Ty's first experience with a law enforcement partner or training officer. The duties were exciting and the very reason he had joined the army. Assignments included working with kids as the school resource officer duties at the American schools. Ty enjoyed this duty as they talked to kids about being in a foreign country and career building. Some of the calls for MP service included dealing with domestic quarrels in base housing and breaking up bar fights in the local towns of Bamberg and Augsburg. Yes, he even got "stick time" (using his baton to subdue drunk soldiers).

Corporal Washington was eager to gain as much experience as possible in the army. He wanted to be a Military Police Investigator (MPI) and/or be assigned to the Criminal Investigation Division (CID). Both MPI and CID were the elite assignments in the Military Police Corps. The downside of these opportunities was that he had only about six months left in the army, and to qualify for CID or MPI, a soldier needed to either extend the tour of duty for an additional two years or have two years left on his current tour. Ty wasn't willing to extend his tour of duty, and this great opportunity with CID passed him by.

White hat MP duty was almost like real police work. In a police sedan labeled "Military Police," Ty patrolled American military compounds. Picking up drunk soldiers from German jails became routine. American soldiers loved to get drunk and start fights with each other and German soldiers. When American soldiers were arrested by German police, they were held in German jails until MPs arrived to take them back to base.

These soldiers were always happy to see army MPs, because the German police, or Polizei, were no-nonsense officers of the law and were respected by all. Any bold, loudmouthed GIs ("government issued" abbreviated, a nickname for American soldiers during World War II) who dared challenge the Polizei never did it twice, because the Polizei beat the shit out of them. One Saturday afternoon, Ty picked up some GIs from the jail in downtown Nuremberg and heard an interesting story.

"Man, all I did was call a German cop a 'kraut pig,' and he beat the shit out of me."

"Learning respect at the end of a nightstick ain't real sweet, is it?" Ty replied.

"No, Corporal, it is not."

Ty's days in Germany went by fast, and his tour of duty was over before he knew it. He walked into the first sergeant's office and picked up his orders, which read, "End Tour Service (ETS)." He was going home. "Back to the world!" Ty said. "California, here I come!"

His last night in Germany was very interesting. Ty took a bus to the Frankfurt Airport, and he was flying home in a civilian aircraft. While waiting for his flight, he drank a few beers in the airport bar. He sat down next to Hans, a German soldier, and a most revealing conversation occurred.

"You know," said Ty, "America is the 'baddest' country in the world. We can kick ass on any country in the world. Not only are we the strongest country in the world, but we are also the most advanced society in the world, including Germany!"

"*Ja*?" replied Hans with a German accent. "You Americans aren't as good as you think! You need to learn manners from other countries in the world on how to treat people. Tell me. How great and wonderful is your America when you, as a Black man, are not free? You're called ugly, degrading names by your fellow Americans and not given the equal treatment and consideration when it comes to jobs, homes, and basic comforts of society. I heard there are places in the southern part of your country where you are still not welcome in restaurants with signs on the door that say, 'Coloreds Enter through the Back Door,' colored drinking fountains, and separate bathrooms!"

Ty was stunned and silent. This German soldier had done his homework.

"How many Black governors are in your country?" Hans continued. "How many Black US senators? You get the message! Don't preach to me about how great America is when your country doesn't even honor the great American statesman Martin Luther King Jr. with a federal holiday."

What could Ty say in response? Normally he was quick with a reply. The German soldier backed Ty and the other American soldiers, who were also Black and White, into a corner.

After a few seconds, Ty said, "How about another beer?"

Nothing more was said. Ty left the table and headed toward the waiting area for his flight.

The bar experience with the German soldier bothered Ty for years. It was 1975, and Ty remembered one Black senator from New Jersey, Edwin Brooke, but no governors and only a few members of Congress.

The army was good for Ty. He matured and developed various skills in education, life, and society. He was going to miss the food, beer, and the beautiful women he had met in Germany. He arrived at the Frankfurt Airport, and after a few hours, he boarded the plane for the inner city. Ty was very excited. Soon he would have a chance to demonstrate the skills he had learned in the army. He was going home, and several hours later, he arrived at LAX. Ty's mother met him. On the way home, he shared his experiences in Germany and talked about his future plans.

SYLVESTER STONE

"Well, Son, now that you have served your country, what are you going to do?" his mom asked him.

"Mom, I still want to be a police officer and prove how valuable Blacks are to American society. I want to be a role model for Black and White America to show Black folks can be more than pimps, drug dealers, gangsters, and welfare recipients. I want to be a Black with a badge."

CHAPTER 3

Rookie Cop: First Black with a Badge

Ty was honorably discharged from the army, and with this great experience, he returned to California to resume the police officer quest. Community college was the first stop; Criminal Law, Evidence, and Community Policing were the first-semester courses. Ty maintained his allegiance to the army by joining the reserves. He had grown accustomed to the military lifestyle and the many skills he learned. Ty had saved some money during his tour in the army; and with this extra money, he rented an apartment near the college, bought a used car, and returned to his quest to become a police officer.

Ty began taking written examinations to become a police officer. His first exam was interesting and started the ball rolling. He walked into a huge auditorium with about three hundred other applicants. They all sat around, very anxious and nervous; suddenly, the exam proctor walked in, gave instructions, and passed out the exams. Two hours later, the applicants completed the English comprehensive and vocabulary test.

Ty and other applicants exited the auditorium and commented on the exam.

"Wow, that test was crazy hard!" said one guy.

"Who cares about right angles?" said another.

"I guess the written exam is to screen out people because there were no police-type questions, only English vocab!" said one more.

Ty wanted to see firsthand about the rumors of how civil service exams were not geared for minorities and why so many failed the written examinations. Maybe this was also why the number of minorities in policing were minimal. Ty failed several of these written examinations. After several months of frustration, Ty passed a written exam. The next step was an oral interview, and in preparation, he contacted his friend Juan, a police officer friend from a nearby city. Juan mentored him through the police oral interview process.

"Listen and pay attention to every question. Be honest. Don't try to bullshit them. If you're unsure, tell them and let them know you will research the answer. Be assertive where you need to be, and remember, you are the best candidate. Emphasize your military service and how you want to continue serving society as a police officer."

Juan showed Ty his police officer badge. "Visualize this as your badge. When you walk into that interview, you must be filled with command presence, confidence, and sincerity."

Ty's mother also helped prepare him for the interview by giving tips on how to dress. "Son, wear a conservative black suit, white shirt, and black tie."

"Thanks, Mom. I really appreciate your support and coaching me through this process."

These were positive, reinforcing mentoring sessions for Ty, where he gained confidence, etiquette, and family values.

He woke early the next morning and put on a nice black suit, white shirt, and black tie. He drove to the interview. He entered the police department to check in for his interview. He was told to wait patiently in the lobby until his name was called. After about thirty minutes, the silence was broken when a gentleman in a neatly pressed gray suit introduced himself to Ty as Investigator Diligent. The investigator escorted him to the interview room, and Ty was introduced to the interview panel.

"Good morning, Mr. Washington. Relax and tell us a little about yourself."

Ty briefly described growing up in the inner city and the local suburb.

"Why do you want to be a police officer, and why should we hire you?"

"I have two years of college, and I believe in the police force working for the community," Ty answered. "Serving the public is the essence of twentieth-century policing. In addition, I served my country in the United States Army, where I learned discipline, decision-making, and individual responsibility."

"Do you believe in affirmative action?"

"Yes, but with conditions. It should be monitored closely to ensure the intent of the law is followed and it is not abused."

"Anything else?" asked the panel.

"Yes, I should be hired because I am a qualified police officer candidate, and I will add value to the entire community."

After forty-five of the longest minutes of his life, the interview ended. As Ty was leaving the room, Diligent told him he'd contact Ty on the results in two weeks; at which time, Investigator Diligent called and told him he had passed the interview and would be scheduled for the next phase of the hiring process.

The next phase of the testing process was the psychological evaluation. Ty reported to the psychologist's office and was asked to complete a five-hundred-question written examination. The questions were odd to Ty. Some were "Do you like flowers and butterflies?" or "Do you often think of things too terrible to talk about?" After the written portion, Ty waited in the lobby for about thirty minutes and was called into the psychiatrist's office. He was face-to-face with a Dr. Behavior, and once he was in the office, the doctor asked him to sit on the couch, and the interview began.

"I have reviewed your test answers," the doctor said. "They indicate to me that you have a high regard for others, and based on these findings, I believe you will make a fine police officer."

They talked for about thirty minutes, at which time the interview was complete. He thanked Ty for his sincerity and wished him the best in the future.

After the psychological exam came the polygraph (lie detector) test. Ty had heard many stories about how lie detector tests were unreliable and geared to screen out minorities. The rumors about the written exam and the polygraph didn't seem to impact Ty as he proceeded through the hiring process. Ty arrived at the examiner's office and sat nervously in the waiting room. He was called into the polygraph room itself, and the examiner hooked him to the machine. The examiner looked like Sergeant Joe Friday from *Dragnet*, with a short flattop haircut, white shirt, black tie, and coat.

"Relax," the examiner said as he began the questioning. "Is your name Tyrone?"

"Yes."

"Have you ever stolen money from an employer?"

"No."

"Have you ever had sex with a donkey or chicken?"

"You've got to be kidding!" Ty sputtered.

The examiner looked at him. "Don't worry. Believe it or not, these questions are all part of the procedure. The needle jumping on the machine is a natural response to such a question. If it didn't jump, we would seriously want to question your personal preferences."

Ty settled in and completed the examination, and two hours later, he left the polygraph examiner's office.

He received the official word the following day on both exams; he had passed both the psychological and polygraph tests.

Next in the process was the physical fitness test. This consisted of dragging a 150-pound dummy one-quarter of a mile around the running track, running one mile, and completing an obstacle course. Ty was in top physical shape after his tour in the army and completed the test in record time.

The last and most important phase of testing was the background investigation. Ty filled out a comprehensive seventy-page document, in which his life information was requested. This included previous employers, friends, and contacts within the criminal justice system. He didn't have a criminal record, so that portion of the investigation was easy. Still, family members and friends were contacted and asked to provide a character reference regarding Ty. Background investigations generally took four to six months to complete; Ty's was completed in three months.

The moment of a lifetime dream was about to be revealed. He received a phone call from the background investigator.

"Congrats, Ty, you have successfully passed the background investigation. Mr. Washington, this is Sergeant Jones from Hometown Police Department. We would like to invite you to a hiring interview with the police chief tomorrow at nine a.m."

"Thank you, sir. I will be there."

The next day, he drove to the police station, and Juan met him and escorted him into the chief's office.

"Mr. Washington," said the chief, "you passed every phase of the testing process, and I would like to offer you a position as a police officer with this department."

"Thank you, sir. I am honored and will do my very best to live up to the high standards of the profession."

"Welcome aboard," the chief said. "Juan will assist you with your introductions and sponsorship to our department. You are the first Black police officer hired in the history of this department. I wish you the best. If you have any problems, let me know. Your academy class starts in two weeks, so you have a little time to prepare."

"No problem, sir, I will be ready."

Ty thanked the chief and walked out of his office.

Juan escorted Ty into his office and began processing to include the uniform purchase order and his start date of the police academy. Ty thanked him, left the office, and drove straight to his parents' house. But first, he made a pit stop. Ty reported to the uniform store and picked up his academy khaki uniforms.

"Mom, I made it! I'm a police officer. I was hired by Hometown Police Department!"

"That's great, Son! Your dream has come true! Be all you can be, but remember, do not trust anyone!"

Next, Ty called Officer Juan, thanking him for the mentoring, coaching, and assistance in achieving his lifelong quest.

"You are welcome, but remember, the academy is tough and challenging. It's like military training but different as well. The focus in the academy is academics. Stay focused, don't give up under any circumstances, and always maintain your command presence and poise because you will face racial harassment."

"Thank you, Juan. The race thing will be new. I am sure there will be training courses on race relations like in the army."

"I do not think so, Ty, but best of luck to you, and again, congrats!"

Ty was on top of the world—a childhood dream had been reached. The stage was set, and now it was time for Ty to work at being the best cop possible. Ty sat in his room and thanked God for allowing him the opportunity to achieve his dream. He realized it was God's grace that had opened this career door.

"Mom, I rented an apartment near the police academy. Thank you for always providing guidance and staying in my face when it was necessary."

"Well, Son, it is time for you to learn how to live on your own. Don't hesitate to call or come by. This is always your home."

He thanked his mom and packed his VW bug with clothes and a few personal items. The academy was about forty miles from his mom's house. For the next two weeks, Ty exercised, worked out, and began reading more articles on policing.

He reported to the academy in his khaki uniform, which displayed a cloth police badge, a Sam Browne gun belt, handcuffs, and an empty gun holster. He met his fellow classmates in the parking lot of the police academy. The recruits represented police departments from across the nation. They stood around in the parking lot and weren't sure where or how to line up. His army experience took center stage.

Ty addressed his classmates, "let's line up like we are in the military. Everyone, let's form four rows and make them even." Some of his fellow classmates were military vets as well and supported Ty in this first police academy formation.

There were ninety new police academy rookies in Ty's class. The demographics of his classmates ranged from military vets to department-store security guards and schoolteachers. The ethnic composition wasn't as diverse as Ty had expected. The class had four White females, three Black males, eight Hispanic males, one Asian, and the rest were White males. These numbers would decrease by graduation.

Police academy training was similar in format and structure to military training, with early-morning wake-up calls, running with the rising sun, and various exercise programs. The academy cadre were like the military drill sergeants; they yelled, wore "Smokey the Bear" hats, and called cadence as the police recruits ran in formation. The recruits had daily formations, uniform inspections, and demerits for poor performance. The transition for Ty was much easier than many of the other police recruits.

The daily curriculum of criminal justice courses was basic but rigid; in a classroom setting, discipline and attention to detail were the standard. The intense eight-hour daily training routine was well balanced and presented in a positive manner. Ty enjoyed the structure; some of the courses covered topics such as criminal law, traffic enforcement, and criminal procedure.

One day in criminal law, a funny thing happened. The instructor asked Recruit Smith, "What are the elements of a robbery?"

"Well, sir, to tell you the truth," Recruit Smith replied, "I don't fucking know, sir!"

Smith was applauded because he had made this comment when the tactical training staff had briefly left the room and left the poor civilian instructor in the classroom. His applause accompanied a roar of laughter from the other recruits. Well, Ty wasn't sure whether it was bravery or stupidity. His little comical moment earned the class five extra miles and a hundred push-ups for the next week.

Despite the rigor, discipline, and constant yelling by the tactical training staff, the police academy was a great life experience. Ty felt like he was part of another family of friends like the military. However, the police academy was where he was introduced to racial slurs and jokes.

One morning in the gym locker room, while preparing for physical fitness training, a couple of fellow recruits asked, "Hey, Ty, why do they call Black people 'jungle bunnies'?"

"I'm not sure," replied Ty.

"Hmm, maybe it is because you boys are slow and not very well educated and still act like you are in the jungles of Africa."

Some of the other recruits laughed and found these comments funny, while others did not.

Ty stood in amazement, and as he started walking away, he heard the recruit say, "Told you niggers aren't that smart. See how he walked away!"

Ty was angry, he stormed out of the room started hitting the lockers. He stopped, turned around and yelled, "If I hear you use that word again, I will kick your ass up and down the academy steps!"

There was silence, and Ty walked away. A new era for Ty had begun. Racial jokes and slurs would define his early years in police work.

One evening during a study session, one recruit asked, "Hey, Ty, did you know that Negroes are living proof that the Indians screwed buffaloes?"

"That's not funny," Ty replied. "In fact, it is very racist and offensive! I have had enough of these stupid racial jokes."

"You'd better get used to them, because if you can't take the racial jokes from fellow officers, how are you going to deal with suspects calling you 'nigger' or 'jungle bunny'?" another recruit commented.

"That is the point," Ty protested. "Fellow officers should not demonstrate racial behavior against me!"

This was his first experience with racial slurs and jokes, which startled Ty. But he felt they were just playful jokes. Maybe that episode was an icebreaker, conversation piece, or coping mechanism for the recruits as they endured the demanding environment of a police academy.

After four months of rigorous training and the occasional racial jokes, the police academy was coming to an end. Only two weeks were left. There was a very high attrition rate, since only forty-five of the original ninety recruits graduated. The minority graduate numbers changed as well. Two out of the original three Blacks, two out of the four females, and three out of the four Hispanics graduated. Ty's individual class standing was good; he was fifth physically and tenth academically out of the forty-five graduating recruits. He completed the academy with an 87 percent overall academy score—not bad for the kid from the inner city.

Graduation day came at last! Ty and his classmates were ready to transition from academy recruits to police officers with a sworn duty to protect and serve their respective cities. The many hours of studying, late nights, and physical fitness training had paid off.

The police graduation was in a large auditorium. The recruits sat on stage in their assigned seats while families sat in the audience. The forty-five police recruits were about to become police officers. Yes, the attrition rate was 50 percent.

The recruits looked sharp in their class A uniforms, long-sleeved shirts and ties, and Sam Browne gun belts with the mace, weapon, baton, handcuffs, and so forth. The only missing items were the individual police department metal badges; as during the entire academy, the recruits wore only generic police academy cloth badges. The recruits wore one additional piece of equipment; the holsters weren't empty since each recruit possessed his or her firearm.

Excitement filled the auditorium as the guest speaker, a local police chief, approached the microphone.

"This is a great day, recruits," the speaker began. "Your determination, desire, and integrity have paid high dividends. It is time to go forth from this place of training and apply those skills you have learned in the academy to protect society."

The chief finished his speech, and the recruits were called up one at a time to have their individual agency metal badges pinned on their uniforms. (There were about eight different police agencies.)

The badge-pinning ceremony was an awesome sight; the recruit's police chief, parent, or significant other pinned the badge on his or her uniform. Ty's mother pinned on his Hometown Police Department badge. The pinning signified the recruits were now police officers. After all badges were pinned, the guest speaker swore the new police officers in, and with this, they were all full-fledged sworn police officers in dark-blue uniforms, not the khaki academy uniforms.

When the ceremony concluded, Ty kissed his mom and took a commemorative picture with his classmates, some of whom he would never see again since they were from different police agencies in the state. He was pleased and happy his mother had attended this important event. The graduating class hosted a party at a local restaurant. The new police officers partied all night into the early morning; it was a joyous event.

Ty woke the next morning with a tremendous hangover and rushed to get dressed for his first day on the job. He was nervous to report to work because the local newspapers had featured him in an article titled "Hometown PD Hires First Black Police Officer."

Upon arriving to the police department, the training sergeant and his new field training officer, Officer Bumper was an experienced, old-school police officer, who was generally considered to be a nice guy. Ty and Bumper sat through roll call, then walked together to the parking lot.

Bumper tossed him the car keys and said, "Okay, son, the car is over there, number seventy-six. The city map is inside the glove compartment. I'll point the way while you drive."

Ty started the car, backed out of the parking space, and exited the parking lot; they were off on the city streets. Officer Tyrone Washington was on patrol. Bumper leaned back in the passenger seat, and Officer Washington drove the police car in his assigned patrol beat.

"Things aren't too bad here," Bumper said to Ty. "Listen, rook, remember to keep your mouth shut. Ask no questions, and you will pass field training and your probation period of one year. Just keep driving until we receive a radio call. No vehicle stops or pedestrian checks—just let me sit here and relax."

They drove around for about an hour, and suddenly the radio came on. "Unit twelve, respond to a one forty three on Lemon Street, burglary past," squawked a voice from the radio.

Bumper told Ty to look at the city map and locate the address. Once he had found it, they drove to the location.

"Okay, kid, go get 'em," Bumper said once they arrived. "Let's see how you do on taking your first report."

They contacted the reporting party.

"Good morning, ma'am. May we help you?" Ty said.

"Yes, someone broke into my home over the weekend and stole my TV, stereo, and jewelry."

"Please provide me with a detailed description of the property taken and include serial numbers if you have them."

Ty completed the report, and they left the location and said to Bumper, "That wasn't so bad. Simple burglary, which I will write and finish in no time. The night is young, and I must approve all your reports before they are submitted to the shift sergeant for approval."

Bumper was right; two traffic collisions and two theft reports rounded out the night for Ty. He completed the reports and turned them into Bumper for review. They completed the shift, and Ty went home.

The next day, he reported to work, checked his department mailbox, and discovered all the reports from the night before had been rejected and required corrections before going to the sergeant.

"Is this normal to have your reports rejected like this for minor discrepancies?" Ty asked Bumper.

"Yes, the reports are written for prosecution and go to the district attorney's office, courts, and other police agencies. Some sergeants are pickier than others, and I don't want to take chances. I want to make sure the reports are perfect! Reports must be clear, concise, and contain all the elements of a crime."

"Okay, I understand, but didn't my reports contain those required elements?"

"For the most part, yes, but there were some grammatical errors," Bumper retorted. "Don't worry, keep working, and the reports will improve. Rookie cops must be careful not to piss off the sergeants by complaining about report rejections. If a new cop pisses off the training officer or sergeant, et cetera, report writing will be used to justify getting rid of the rookie cop. I don't think you have to worry about report rejections. Just listen to what I teach you, and you will have no problems with your reports."

"Sounds great. Thanks, Bumper!"

In the following weeks, many of Ty's reports were rejected or returned for minor corrections. He had good days and bad days, and the bad days centered on report rejection. He learned report rejection—the infamous red-ink pen corrections—were a real but very negative aspect of policing. It was necessary to reject and correct reports, but Ty would later learn this process was also used as a weapon of termination.

Ty and Bumper worked diligently on his report writing, and finally after months, the reports were satisfactory. Ty completed the field training officer program. Police patrol was the foundation of policing, and report writing was one of the most important functions.

Ty called his mom to let her know how training was going; as always she issued a warning. "Son, racial jokes and slurs are a common occurrence. Whites today still openly use the words *nigger*, *spook*, *porch monkey*, and other racial epithets to describe Black people. Tolerating this behavior by laughing at the racial slurs was a true survival mechanism for Black and other minority police officers. Caution: if you stand up and detest the jokes and slurs, hollering it is your right as an American to be treated fairly, you will be doomed to isolation, discipline, and termination. I only want what is best for you."

CHAPTER 4

Implicit Bias from Within

Now with only three months on the job, the atmosphere changed. Ty reported to work one Saturday afternoon and discovered a cartoon cutout on his wall locker in the police department locker room. The cartoon depicted a Black character standing in front of white-hooded Ku Klux Klan members; they were handing the Black man a cake with cross-shaped burning candles, which included another Klansman holding a rope, shaped like a tie.

This cartoon depicted a time in American history when Black men had been lynched. Some Black homes had burning crosses placed in their front yards. He ripped the cartoon off his wall locker and took it to Bumper, who was down the hall. Ty showed him the cartoon and said, "What kind of shit is this?"

"I don't know, Ty. I certainly didn't pin it on your wall locker."

Ty walked away, returned to the locker room, and got dressed for roll call. While sitting there, he looked around to see whether anyone was smiling or would admit to the practical joke. No one said anything. The sergeant concluded roll call and issued the officers their assignments. Everyone left the room. Ty was on probation and could be fired for no cause, so he kept silent about this racial cartoon. He finished his patrol shift and went home to his apartment.

He called a couple of friends. "Hey, Charlie, you won't believe what happened today. Someone at the police station taped a racist cartoon on my wall locker, showing a Black man being given a cake with burning cross candles and a rope in one hand!"

"Wow, Ty, that is some racist shit!" Charlie said.

"White folks just won't change! Who did that?"

"Don't know. If I were you Ty, I would let it slide and work on passing probation."

The significance of this cartoon was degrading, since the KKK had a more than hundred-year history of specifically terrorizing Blacks and other minorities, including Jewish people. The KKK were historically known for lynching or hanging Blacks for no other reason than being Black. Despite the humiliation and demeaning message in the cartoon, Ty marched forward and worked hard to be a good cop. There was no investigation when Ty brought this comic to light with his training officer.

One aspect of his job he loved was visiting the schools in the city and talking to kids about gangs and drugs. He remembered seeing drug addicts in the alleys of the inner city (ghetto) as a kid and gangsters hanging out at the park. Ty had become a cop to change this image and help young kids not become gangsters and engaged in drugs.

Ty visited the local community center to talk with some of the local gangsters who were hanging out.

"*Que Paso, Ese?*" (What's going on, dude?) one gang member said to him.

"Same old stuff. Just keeping the peace. And you, *vato*, my dude?"

"Kicking it, homes, just relaxing."

"Remember, stay in school, work hard, do the right thing, and be faithful to yourself. This thug life you're leading will end someday, and then where will you guys be? Hold your heads up high and do the right thing," Ty said. "Okay, gotta split. Take it easy, catch you guys later."

Ty left the center, hoping he'd made a positive impression on the gang members about police.

He enjoyed mentoring and talking with the young people in the community. He wanted to be a role model and show them he had grown up around gangs and drugs, but they hadn't stopped him from becoming a police officer. He told the young men that their choices determined their future, not necessarily where they lived.

"It doesn't matter if you live in the ghetto or barrio," Ty taught. "You can become successful. Being poor is not an excuse to not work hard, study, and go to school. You must always believe in yourself and work hard."

Two weeks later, Ty responded to a disturbance call at the community center; he was one of many officers who arrived at the scene. During the disturbance, most of the police cars were damaged by rocks and bottles. The only police car untouched by rocks and bottles was Ty's.

"Hey, Ty, how is it your police car didn't get hit with rocks and bottles?" one officer asked.

"I guess the kids respect me because I'm not always calling them assholes or other racist names like some of you do."

"Whatever," replied the officer as he got into his rock-damaged police car.

A couple of days went by. Ty returned to the community center to talk with a few known gang members about the disturbance.

"Hey, Ese, why do those White cops always insult us, calling us 'beaners,' 'wetbacks,' or 'greasers' because we are Mexican?" one of the gangsters asked him. "That shit ain't right."

"You are right. I will talk to some of the officers, but I am not responsible for their actions, especially since I am a new rookie cop."

"True that, homey, but you are respectful to us, and we respect you."

Ty departed the center, ended his shift, and went home.

While watching TV at home, he thought about what had happened at the center. He understood how it felt to receive racial slurs, even as recently as a few weeks prior when the racial cartoon had been placed on his wall locker. He thought, *If my fellow officers are racist to me by the slurs, jokes, and gestures, what chance do the minority kids at the center have?*

The next morning, Ty arrived at work and found another racist paper inside his police department mailbox. The cartoon depicted a Hispanic gang member with a bull's-eye target sight on it with a caption that said, "Pachuco," a name common to Hispanic males in the '70s. Why did he receive this in his mailbox? It hit Ty that a few days after the rock-and-bottle incident, all police cars but his were damaged; that was probably why he had been singled out. He ignored this leaflet and began his patrol shift.

Ty received a radio call. "Unit eleven, return to the station and contact the dispatcher."

He arrived at the station and reported to the dispatcher's office, where Sergeant Mystery met him and said, "Some of the guys bought you lunch to show there are no hard feelings between officers on this shift."

Ty walked into the roll call room and saw a slice of watermelon sitting on a table.

"See, Ty," replied the sergeant, "no hard feelings."

The other officers started laughing and telling Ty to relax and lighten up and not be so uptight.

"Don't be upset," one officer said. "We know this is the national food of your people. We just want to make you feel at home."

Ty shook his head in disbelief, walked out of the room, and returned to his police car. He finished his patrol shift and went home. These were the times his mom had warned him about. Ty prayed for strength and remembered his mom's words. "Be strong, Son, and do not let them turn you around."

Ty understood he was the only Black officer in the department of fifty-five officers, where there were a handful of Hispanic and female officers, but most of the entire department was White. The watermelon incident reminded Ty that it was Sergeant Mystery who frequently rejected his reports and loved telling racial jokes.

At the end of his shift, he changed clothes.

"Ty, you have to maintain a sense of humor to be a good cop," said one of the officers as he approached Ty, who was walking out the back door of the police department. "I know the racial jokes cannot be easy to listen to, but remember, in policing there is an acceptance ritual for all new cops. You are no different. It just so happens race is the easiest ritual prank to pull on you. The guys are breaking the ice with you. Things will get better. After all, these are the same guys you have to depend on to back you up in dangerous situations and save your life."

"You know," replied Ty, "I am not sure these same racial joke tellers will have my back!"

He turned and walked away from the officer, entered his car, and drove away.

Later in the week while patrolling, he stopped at the local coffee shop. Two other officers were also getting coffee and asked him, "Hey, are you still upset over that watermelon joke? Hell, we thought all you people liked watermelon and thought it would be a funny joke."

"No, man, it wasn't funny. Can't you guys find better things to do with your time? And do all the jokes have to be racial?"

"Well, there is so much material, and the racial stuff is really funny."

Ty bought his coffee and returned to patrol.

He began to think about the constant racial harassment and sought support from his supervisor. Ty returned to the station and approached his sergeant. "Sergeant Mystery?"

"Yes?" replied the sergeant.

"How do I deal with the constant racial jokes? They are very distracting and impact my job performance."

"Well, Ty, as for your reports, if you'd write with a pencil and not a spear, your reports might improve." He laughed, handed Ty some rejected reports, and told him to return to his patrol duties.

Ty returned to patrol, finished his shift, and drove home. He was above angry, but there was no one on the department to support him, because no one believed there was a problem. The actions of many of the officers and sergeants were simply that of breaking in a new rookie cop who happened to be Black. Ty just wanted to make probation and be a regular cop, yet his gut told him the racial harassment he was experiencing was wrong. But to whom would he complain?

Ty called his friend, Officer Bay.

"Listen, I am getting racial slurs and jokes from the officers, including sergeants!" Ty said. "How am I supposed to learn about police work when this shit is a weekly occurrence? I understand there are no laws protecting me. So much for the progressive seventies!"

"Ty, sorry, I know this is hard, but you must get through probation because you can be terminated without cause. Hang in there. It will get better once you get through probation."

"Thank you," Ty replied.

Ty sat in his living room, watching *Adam-12* and wondering why racial harassment hadn't been discussed in the police academy or in any of his college courses. He was midway through the probation period and nearly six months on the department and wondered whether he would pass probation. Ty felt he was being targeted for failure, and as the probation period was nearly over, he would be terminated.

It is typical in many cases for probationary officers to be terminated for not meeting standards. In Ty's case, he believed race would be the determining factor for him, not the constant rejection of his reports. He believed the report rejection would be the rationalization to terminate him. He was determined to succeed, so in his final few months, Ty enrolled in an English composition class to improve his report writing.

He returned to work after two relaxing days off, when he visited some friends at the local beach. He walked into the locker room and noticed another racial sight. All the lockers around his locker had signs on them, which said, "For Sale by Owner." This was a well-known expression by White homeowners in the '50s, '60s, and '70s. The message was, as Blacks moved in, Whites moved out; the common term was "White flight."

Why do these officers continue to do this? Because I am the only Black officer? Ty thought. *Why would the other officers stand by and let this continue? Because they are White? Why am I not accepted at this police department?*

Ty needed a strategy to fight back, but what was it? The pressure was mounting. His reports were still being rejected, and his depression prevented his concentration at work, and another nail was put in his professional coffin—a negative performance evaluation. He reached out to some Black officers in other agencies, and while the meetings were being set up, he continued at Hometown PD.

Christmas was approaching, but what holiday cheer would they bring Ty? Ty received his answer upon arriving to work one Sunday afternoon. He put on his uniform and reported to roll call. It was so far so good, since no derogatory flyers or leaflets had been pinned on his locker. After roll call, he checked his department mailbox, and boom, there was another racial flyer. This one depicted a Black Santa Claus crawling out the window of a home, carrying a bag over his back filled with stolen items from the house. The message was, "Blacks are crooks and burglars, even a Black Santa Claus."

The officers from the other agencies met Ty, along with some Mexican-American officers. Ty asked whether they received racial jokes and slurs. Most said yes, and a few said no. One of the officers asked him whether the "For Sale by Owner" prank really happened.

"Yes, it did," Ty said.

"Hey, man, we heard those racist assholes haven't stopped. It looks like they really enjoy harassing you."

"Yeah, the shit doesn't stop. Every now and then no jokes, comments, or slurs for a few weeks, and then *bam*! It starts again. How do you guys deal with racial jokes?"

"I don't put up with it," commented Willie, one of the minority officers. "The minute I hear a racist joke or slur, I shut it down immediately and follow it with a complaint to the sergeant. If he doesn't respond, I contact the lieutenant and go all the way up the chain of command to the chief, if necessary."

"Yeah," added Officer Concern. "You have to let them know you will not tolerate their racist, unethical conduct. If you don't, they'll never stop."

71

"You guys can do that because there is strength in numbers," Ty countered. "I am the only one, and the very people I would appeal to are White as well. Furthermore, I want to pass probation and keep my job. If I start filing complaints, they will retaliate and fire me. This is the 1980s, and things are not that much better."

"Hey, you may get fired anyway," one officer said.

"We hear you, Ty. Let me guess how things are for you. Your reports are rejected for minor mistakes, the sergeants are saying you need to improve your performance, and you are below standard."

"How did you know?"

"I experienced the same harassment at my agency until I put my foot down. It's so distracting and interferes with learning the job as a cop. I do not put up with any of the racial nonsense.

"You know, Ty, I have been in law enforcement for about twelve years, and it is common for rookie cops to write poor reports, and the department has an obligation to assist and support officers with poor report-writing skills to help them improve!

"Keep the faith," Officer Concern added. "Remember why you wanted to become a cop in the first place. Maybe someday you'll be in charge and have the power to change the negative, racist behavioral traits of others in policing."

Ty smiled and thanked his friends, and after a couple of hours, they all went home.

Another day at the office. When Ty walked into the locker room and was getting dressed, one of the officers said to him, "Hey, Ty, why do you jungle bunnies—I mean, Black guys—run so fast?"

"That's a stupid question," Ty replied.

"Really? Okay, how about this. Why do *you people* like Ultra Sheen and watermelon?"

"Another dumb, stupid, and racist comment."

Saturated by months of racial harassment and torture in his mind, he finally lost his cool and snapped at the officer. "When will this shit stop? Day after day I must listen to these degrading racial jokes and slurs! If half the effort was placed into helping me write better reports, things might be better for me here!"

"Your reports are fine," the officer replied, intimidated, surprised at Ty's outburst, remembering he and Ty were alone in the locker room. "The report rejections, racial jokes, and slurs were our response to having a Black officer shoved down our throats. All this affirmative action bullshit upset many of the officers. Because of you, our department was placed in the county limelight, a light we didn't want or ask for!"

"Wow, that is one hell of a confession," Ty replied. "This wasn't my fault. I just wanted to be a good cop!"

"Sorry, Ty," the officer said as he left the locker room.

Ty finished getting dressed, went to roll call, and started his patrol shift. The shift ended without incident, and he went home and got a good night's sleep.

One week passed, and there were no incidents. Ty came to work early to review his reports and discovered another racial leaflet in his department mailbox. It was a police crime report completely filled out with racially degrading comments. In its various sections report section, it should have said, Crime Section: Kidnapping but the report read,

"Crime Section: Nigger-napping / Location: City Jail / Method Operandi: Locked up for safe keeping. Summary: Nigger found to have arrest warrants and taken into custody and placed in safest place possible, jail."

Someone had taken the time to fill out a state-certified police crime report form with these racial epithets. This leaflet truly illustrated the level of maliciousness of the officers in his department. They had even violated the law by this unauthorized and illegal use of a state-certified crime report.

What brought this on? thought Ty. *Hmm, a week earlier, I arrested a young Black male for warrants and booked him into the city jail. The arrest was questionable, in that there may not have been sufficient probable cause.*

But Ty wanted to be accepted by his peers at the expense of this young Black male. This was a moment of self-reflection, because he realized this hadn't been the best judgment call by him, and he couldn't let the stress and frustration cause him to exercise such poor judgment.

The next day in roll call, one of the officers said, "Hey, Ty, are you gonna kidnap any more colored boys?"

"Yeah," shouted another officer. "Yeah, keep arresting them. The crime rate in town will go down!"

Enough was enough. Ty had to take a stand.

"Knock it off!" commented the watch commander, Sergeant Verbal.

After roll call, Ty approached Sergeant Verbal, thinking he would support him.

"Sir, why the hell do the officers think the telling of racial jokes and slurs is okay? Sir, this shit is not funny. I am sick of it! It stops now!"

"Come on, Ty, you have to have a sense of humor in this business and not take everything so personal," Sergeant Bob responded. "That's part of being a good cop and being accepted into the brotherhood."

"Bullshit, sir."

Ty left the sergeant's office and started his shift. It was a positive night of two arrests, two reports, and no rejections!

As Ty thought about his daily situation, he found it very curious the racial slurs that came from brother cops. Very seldom did he receive racial epithets from citizens he arrested. Where were the ethics? The professionalism and the proud heritage embodied in police work? The term *hostile work environment* was in its infancy. There was no procedural due process to resolve racial harassment grievances. There was the Police Officer Association (POA), a union-type organization in police departments that represented police officers. The only problem was, the association was composed of the same officers making the racial slurs. There was no due process protection for Officer Tyrone Washington.

Who could he turn to for advice? Mom? Dad? Brothers? Who? Ty returned to the Lord. He gave his burdens to God for support and sanctuary. He began regularly attending church again. He had been raised in the church, and his mom had always told him about the power of Jesus.

CHAPTER 5

Battered on the Beat
Hometown PD

Ty's dream was quickly becoming a nightmare. He needed moral support in the worst way. Becoming a police officer had been his lifelong dream, but it appeared to be going up in a racial rhetoric fire. He reached out to some Black police officers from Metropolitan Police Department and traveled to Texas to attend the National Organization of Black Law Enforcement Executives (NOBLE) workshop. NOBLE had been in existence for only a few years, and Ty sought support and refuge.

There were many speakers at this workshop; the topics varied. Ty noticed a pattern in the treatment of minority police officers, especially Black ones. Report writing, he learned, was used as a tool to evaluate, discipline, and terminate many Black, Hispanic, and female officers. This fact alarmed him, and he talked to a metro sergeant.

"Sarge, I have been the victim of constant report rejection, and at the same time I've hammered by racial slurs and jokes. What do I do?"

"You can't let it get to you," Sergeant Gibbs replied. "Black cops are in a fishbowl—our every move is scrutinized and second-guessed. Believe me, I understand! It is generally known among us Blacks that we cannot just meet the standard—we must exceed it. You are not White, so do not expect to be treated as an equal. White cops can make attitude arrests, use excessive force with impunity, and it is accepted. You cannot. The system isn't fair. I have faith in our profession of policing. Maybe someday we may even see a Black police chief. After fifteen years on the job, I don't see any changes in the blatant racist attitudes of some White police officers."

A lieutenant overheard the conversation and said, "White cops do not want an educated, articulate, or verbal Black man—in other words, a truly sharp Black cop. They want a 'steppin' fetchin'' or a 'yes, um" negro—a Black cop who doesn't complain about the racial jokes but laughs and accepts the racial degradation. The kind of Black cop who does whatever he or she is told to do without question and never complains. Let me say this to you. Keep your opinions to yourself to avoid being labeled a 'mouthy brother,' but you know you are not called a Negro. Once you receive this label, the countdown to disciplinary action and termination begins.

"Ty, I realize you are the lone ranger, the only Black at your department," the lieutenant continued. "Therefore, it is so important not to react to the harassment. If you were here at Metropolitan PD, your support group would be much greater—you wouldn't be alone. The Black Police Officers Association was formed to support the concerns and issues of Black police officers in your same situation."

"Wow, how cool is that! An association to support and mentor Blacks."

"Ty, I have another tip for you. Do not let the verbal abusers see you are bothered by the racial slurs and jokes. They are like piranha. If they smell blood in the water, they will attack."

"Too late," replied Ty. "I have become so fed up, I've started rebelling at every joke or slur made. I know I should have been cooler, but I cannot bear this harassment any longer. I have no support groups or friends on the agency. The stress is overwhelming."

The one-day workshop concluded. Ty was energized; for the first time in his short law enforcement career, he didn't feel alone. He understood the approach—one day at a time.

He returned home and stopped for lunch at a local restaurant in the city where he worked. One of his fellow city police officers walked in and approached Ty. "Be careful about eating those hotdogs," the officer said. "Are you sure ribs wouldn't be better for you? By the way, what do Kinney Shoes and Hughes Aircraft have in common?"

"What?" replied Ty.

"Thirty thousand black loafers!"

The officer picked up his to-go order and left the restaurant, laughing. Ty finished his meal and reported to work.

I guess it's not going to change, Ty thought. *I'm just going to suck it up and stay the course. Much easier said than done.*

Ty walked into roll call, received his assignment, walked out to the parking lot, and began loading his patrol car. He began his daily patrol duties, and it was a slow day.

The silent calm of the Sunday morning was broken by a radio transmission. "Unit seventeen, I'll be making a Jefferson stop at First and Main."

This wasn't the first time he had heard this unfamiliar radio transmission, and before he could acknowledge it, another officer answered and responded to the location. "Proceeding to the area," Ty also radioed.

"Negative. Do not respond," the sergeant radioed. "We have sufficient police cars in the area."

Later, Ty asked another officer, "What is a Jefferson stop?" It wasn't in the radio code book.

"Forget about it," the officer said. "Those are rare radio transmissions."

A couple of days passed, and Ty continued asking other officers about warrant subjects.

"Fine. You asked," replied Officer John. "A warrant subject is code for stopping Black guys. Because you know and understand, a backup officer is always needed when stopping Black guys."

Ty discovered this unwritten code has been around for years. He also discovered other police agencies had a similar type of unpublished code when stopping Blacks. One agency called it a "Charlie stop" when the police stopped a Black person.

He continued patrol and pulled into the parking lot of a convenience store to pick up some snacks. A man ran into the store. "Officer, Officer, a lady is lying on the sidewalk outside," the man said. "It looks like she needs help."

He ran outside and noticed the woman wasn't breathing. He radioed dispatch and advised he was giving CPR to a nonresponsive female in front of the convenience store and to roll paramedics. It seemed like a lifetime waiting on the paramedics; it was the longest three minutes Ty had waited. They finally arrived, took over CPR, and placed the female on a respirator.

Ty was credited with saving her life. This recognition gave Ty a great feeling. "Protect and serve" took on a genuine meaning to him. He finally felt like he was a cop.

Officer Ty Washington walked into the station near the end of his shift, and the shift sergeant contacted him and said, "The chief wants to see you."

Ty immediately walked into the chief's office.

"I've heard some stories about racial slurs and jokes," the chief said. "I can write a directive forbidding this behavior."

"Thanks, Chief, but if you do that, the officers will never trust or accept me. Sir, you cannot order people not to be racist. Thank you, but I will do this on my own."

He left the chief's office. He was very appreciative of the chief's gesture.

Ty struggled to improve on his reports and ignore the continued racial slurs. He called Paul, another friend, who was the only Black officer in his small agency.

"Did you know about 'Jefferson stops'?" Ty asked.

"Yes, why?"

"Because I was introduced to that term a few days ago at my department while I was on patrol. It is a radio code that lets everyone on the radio that day know a Black person is being pulled over on a traffic stop."

"Ty, I never discussed this with you because I was sure that kind of shit had stopped and true professionalism would rule the day. Obviously, I was wrong. Be careful.

You have clearly been targeted. Now you know their secret code word."

"Thank you, Paul. I will stay the course. Talk later."

After nearly one year at Hometown PD, it was probation performance review time to determine whether Ty was going to make it through probation and become a full-time police officer. Corporal Bumper handed Ty his performance review. The report indicated he needed some improvement in his report writing, was a marginal officer, and required close supervision.

"That's great," he muttered to himself. "I have been the recipient of racial slurs and jokes by supervisors and officers for nearly a year with little support or constructive assistance, and *I'm* the one with the negative attitude."

He asked Bumper why the report was so negative.

"Some of the supervisors feel you have a chip on your shoulder about being Black," he replied.

"No shit!" replied Ty. "Do you think the racial slurs and jokes may have affected me, Bumper? I have been subjected to racial harassment from the start, and no one gave a shit."

"We must look at the evaluation report and not cloud it with allegations of racial prejudice," Bumper said.

But as Ty received his notice of personnel action, he actually found out he had passed probation. Ty thanked Bumper and continued working to improve his report writing and be more positive despite the hostile work environment. Ty felt pretty good. He finished his shift and celebrated passing probation with a few cop friends at a local restaurant.

"Congrats, Ty. I know you thought racism would fail you, but it didn't," Officer Sam commented.

"True, but it was a difficult year, and I know the slurs are not going to stop."

"Be careful. I think they are setting you up," Officer Juan said, expressing a different view to Ty. "No one makes continued racial slurs and jokes and then just accepts you as one of the boys."

"Maybe you are right," Ty responded. "But I am going to live for the moment and strive to do my best and improve my performance."

"Cheers." The three toasted and finished their beers.

They finished the get-together, and Ty drove home.

Another workday arrived, and a proud Tyrone swaggered into the locker room, dressed out, and checked his department mailbox. He found another racist paper in his mailbox. The paper was a job application, marked "Simplified Form for Minority Applicants." Stunned, he stood there, holding the offensive form while several other officers stood in the hallway, laughing.

Clutching it angrily, he could hear them laugh and told them, "This shit ain't funny."

The document was very demeaning, derogatory, and highly defamatory about Black and Hispanics when completing a job application. Several of the stereotypes about Blacks and Hispanics were used—from being on welfare to drinking Kool-Aid and eating tortillas and beans as a national food.

"Don't be a poor sport," commented Officer Straight. "Come on, Ty, laugh with us so we know you're cool with jokes."

"Yeah," Officer Smith chimed in. "We want cops who are tough, not thin-skinned, and must be able to take jokes."

"Why don't you guys put this much effort into really being brother cops by stopping the stupid racial jokes and sharing police stories and advice with me?"

"Because it is not our style," Officer Straight said. "We don't believe in affirmative action or any of that liberal freedom shit for minorities and women. It has forced us to accept all of you less qualified minority officers. There's enough of that liberal shit in America today, and we as cops don't have to be. Most of you people are on welfare anyway."

"Slow down, cowboy, with your stereotyped generalizations about minorities. Exactly what do you mean by saying 'you people'?"

"You know damn well what I mean—niggers," Officer Innocent added. "You came here to our PD. We didn't ask for you. We have received media attention simply because we hired a Black cop."

"Hey, I just wanted to be a cop. I'm not looking for any publicity," Ty responded. "I am looking for fair treatment in an environment free of racial hostility. You racist assholes won't let me learn how to be a cop. You won't support me or allow me simple cop fellowship."

With that, he walked away.

Isolation was setting in, and depression was increasing. Ty continued taking his college courses and reaching out to some fellow minority officers for support. Being a cop was taking its toll on Ty. The college was supposed to improve the report writing and overall understanding of policing. He was learning, but some aspects of the job weren't written and impacted him daily. One of those unwritten policies was the police officer's unwritten "code of silence," which appeared to apply only to White male officers. When one of them screwed up, minimum discipline was administered; when it was Ty, the full extent of discipline was administered.

One of the ways Ty relieved stress was to sit by the pier at the beach and just meditate on the stress of living and how policing was strongly influencing his life. He sat in the sand, thinking and wondering.

I wonder how Jackie Robinson dealt with his teammates on the baseball team or Jim Harris in football, Ty pondered. *Both were early pioneers in their respective sports like me in policing. I am the only Black police officer, and the pressure hasn't stopped. I can't give up the fight. Someday policing will not be as hostile to Blacks in the future. I know from watching TV how difficult it was for Dr. King, Rosa Parks, and Cesar Chavez. Guess I should go home and try to sleep. Tomorrow is another day at work. Woo! I do not want to go.*

He left the beach and went home.

Yes, another day at work, and another racial leaflet was in Ty's department mailbox.

Ironically, it was an actual police training document about the KKK, but no one else in the department had received it. Only Ty. The joking purpose of this was to try to either intimidate him or chase him away. Just looking at this document with the Ku Klux Klan was terrifying, yet it invoked extreme anger in Ty.

He was building quite a collection of racial documents, which he held onto because no one would believe his stories about the constant hostile racial environment he experienced in policing. Nevertheless, Ty continued performing his patrol duties, making arrests, writing tickets, and developing community policing contacts. He didn't regret his decision to become a police officer, but he began questioning his dream.

The slogan "Protect and Serve" was crumbling before his eyes in a cloud of racism. Generally, police agencies had unions or associations that supported and protected officers from becoming victims of management misconduct and harassment. But in Ty's case, they were futile. The union members were the same White officers making the racial jokes and slurs. As a result, he didn't feel the traditional police unions and associations would adequately represent his issues.

He met his friend Paul again for coffee.

Paul said, "You know, most traditional POAs believe minority associations such as the Latino Peace Officers or Black Police Officers Association are radical groups by the administrators of the individual police departments. This is not true. Minority associations provide a valuable resource and support base for minority police officers."

Ty didn't want to burden his mother with the stress of work but finally reached out to his mom after meeting with Paul.

"Mom, I cannot stand the constant racial jokes. They consume my time and prevent me from truly learning police work. My time is spent wondering where the next racial assault will come from. I really don't know what to do."

"Son, you're *not* one of them! Remember, I warned you about being the Jackie Robinson at this police department."

"Mom, I thought it was different now. That Jim Crow and the racial hostility it generated was in years gone by."

"Son, no, it has just taken a new form, but it's the same old racist song."

"Mom, I just wanted to be a good cop and be accepted by my fellow police officers. Is that too much to ask for?"

"Son, you cannot control the behavior of others. Racism has been in the history of this country, and only time will heal the wounds of racial degradation. I cannot offer you much more. If you stay, it will continue. I know you have bills and cannot quit. I will continue to pray for you."

"Thanks, Mom."

He left his mom's house and returned to his apartment.

Ty called another Black cop friend. "Hey, Bill, how do you handle racial slurs and jokes?"

"It's simple, man. Birds of a feather flock together. You wanted to be a cop and had to realize that being a Black cop currently is a difficult undertaking."

"Yes, I know, I expect the shit from the public, not from my own fellow police officers."

"Life is not fair," his friend Bill said. "I wish you well, my brother."

Ty had already experienced the support of NOBLE, the National Organization of Black Law Enforcement Executives, which was composed of command executive–level Black law enforcement officials nationwide.

This is a new organization still finding its way in law enforcement, Ty thought. *I believe it will be a valuable resource for all minorities in the future. The purpose of NOBLE is to provide a comfortable and trusting resource of information for minority police officers.*

Ty returned to the inner city and attended another training conference; this time, the event was a two-day session. Several workshops and speakers made presentations. One speaker stood out to him, Captain Mitchell, a young Black police executive from a major non-California city police department. Ty sat in on the workshop attended by about seventy-five persons.

"Good evening, my fellow brothers and sisters in law enforcement," Captain Mitchell said. "It isn't often you have so many Black people together and not have it called an unlawful assembly."

The crowd laughed.

"Seriously, how many of you have been the victims of racial slurs like the one I just made?" the speaker continued. "We are always reminded by our White colleagues that they didn't own slaves and that the Civil War ended years ago. No one is blaming them in 1984 for the continued negative racial atmosphere in America. I told that joke on purpose to illustrate a point. This type of behavior has to change.

"This can only be accomplished through our young, new, and energetic minority police officers. I remember not so long ago that Black officers were only allowed to patrol in Black neighborhoods. Not only were they not assigned patrol beats in the White neighborhoods, but department policy prohibited Black officers from patrolling those areas."

Mitchell took a deep breath and looked around the room.

"Then things began to change. About one year after the Civil Rights Act of 1964 became law, Blacks were allowed to patrol the entire city, not just the Black areas. Let's talk about promotions, assignments, and career progression. The number of Black police executives is constantly rising, and hopefully some of you in this audience will one day become police chiefs."

Applause swept the room, forcing Mitchell to pause before continuing.

"Yes, we are making good progress, but the battle is far from over. I hear the stories of how some of our White colleagues still use the word *nigger* and tell racist jokes and slurs on a constant basis.

"Let me tell you how I would deal with racial jokes. Don't laugh or go along with the malicious, racist humor. Minority police managers should never turn their backs when they hear about such incidents but rather extend the hand of support to deal with this misconduct."

The audience clapped once again.

"These preventative recommendations on dealing with this issue are to minimize the impact of a hostile work environment. Your goal is to learn how to be a cop, learn the importance of concepts like community-oriented policing, obtain graduate college degrees, and attend as many law enforcement service schools as possible. The atmosphere of racial slurs will disrupt and impede the learning of police work, but you must never give up. Dr. King, Rosa Parks, the Kennedy Brothers, and Cesar Chavez all advocated for civil human rights. How many of you have been told you have an attitude problem or are too thin-skinned and need to laugh at the jokes to be accepted?"

Most of the hands in the audience were raised high.

"As Blacks achieve more success in the professional world, remember, you will always be closely monitored," Captain Mitchell continued. "And in some cases, deterred from promotion and positive career progression. Remember, you cannot meet the standard—you must *exceed* the standard at all costs. Change is a dish best served slowly. We must give our White brethren in blue a chance to feel comfortable with having Blacks as partners and leaders in policing.

"I know the hour is late," Mitchell said, glancing at his watch, "but please allow me to add just a bit more. A Black man with an education is a threat to White male dominance, especially in police work. Know it, don't preach it. For illustration purposes only, here is another slur I heard recently. 'What do you call a Black person with a PhD? A nigga, not doctor, as our colleagues are called.'

"Achieving academic success should be the goal of everyone in this room, especially if you want to change the landscape of policing in this country. In other words, no matter how hard we work or how high we go in the social classification, we are still just Black folk to some. I bet if a Black person ever became president of the United States, some would still call him or her that—Black.

"Finally, be smart enough to analyze your department. Know who the players are and whether or not they are professionals or simply wearing the badge for ego's sake. Ethics and professional conduct are the essence of our profession and must be adhered to at all costs. If you identify an ego person with the badge, be careful and remain vigilant of your every word. A professional police leader will support you regardless of color, and they do exist.

"Racial slurs, jokes, and other forms of discrimination practices have no place in policing. We are no longer 'house niggas,' plantation folk, street hoodlums, welfare recipients, or criminals. We too are police professionals! Thank you."

The audience erupted in a steady stream of applause and a well-deserved standing ovation.

The conference was an astounding experience for Ty; again, he felt better about being a cop and wanted to stay the course, no matter what. At last, the years of stress and tension experienced by Black police officers were addressed. The interaction with other Black officers and Captain Mitchell was mental therapy.

Ty had been quietly applying at other police departments to escape the hostile environment of Hometown PD. In addition, he continued attending college to enhance career progression. After several months of applying and interviewing, he was hired by Country PD. He resigned from Hometown to start a new life and career.

Near the end of his time at Hometown PD, Ty met a young waitress, Diane, at the local Marie Callender's restaurant. The relationship developed, and he now had a girlfriend to share in his life. In their numerous conversations, she commented about how difficult it must be for Black police officers.

"I know we have only been dating a few months," she said, "but I am attracted to you because you are a cop and represent the good people in our society. I am saddened by your negative experiences with racism."

"Thank you. The sad part is, I have always wanted to be a cop and serve society in a positive manner. I didn't realize how racist the internal police system would be to one of its own."

CHAPTER 6

Affirmative Inaction
Country PD

Ty's relationship with his girlfriend, Diane, continued to grow until marriage was discussed, and two years later, they were married. During the marriage, they had two beautiful daughters. As a father, he had an obligation to control and monitor the values and habits within his household. He didn't want his children to experience the painful hurt of racism. Ty needed to supplement his income and joined the Army National Guard.

Country PD hired him, and he said goodbye to the trauma and horrible life at Hometown PD. The first day reporting in was always interesting. He just wasn't sure about the reception, and first impressions were important. He reported to the new police department and introduced himself to the desk sergeant.

"Morning, Sergeant. I'm Tyrone Washington, a newly hired lateral transfer officer."

"Hello there, my name is Sergeant Veteran. Welcome to Country PD. You will be assigned a training officer. I understand you are an experienced officer, and although every department is different, I expect you to do well. Here are your department door keys, mailbox number, and locker assignment. Report in tomorrow at 0700. Officer Jones is your assigned field training officer (FTO)."

Ty woke up early and drove in for his first day at Country PD. He met Officer Sincere, and what a surprise! Sincere was Black!

"So," commented Ty, "how did you end up here?"

"Well, brother man, long story, but we can discuss later. Let's get you on the right track for training."

"Sounds great. Let's get started."

"You will hear racial slurs," Officer Sincere said. "Try not to react, and the good ole' boys will leave you alone. If they see it bothers you, it could be a long year for you."

"I understand, but I have experienced this before, and things didn't go well."

"Don't worry. This is your first day. You will learn how to deal with different officers and supervisors. I don't want you to get a jacket of being race sensitive or thin-skinned. Some officers will exploit this because they see it as a weakness. You know cops cannot be seen or perceived as weak."

"I get it. Okay, thanks."

"Ty, while we are discussing this issue right off the bat, be careful which sergeants you turn your reports in to. Some are very picky, and you may perceive them as racist. I have been here four years. Believe me, do not react too fast to the racial slurs. I say this because sometimes it is the very sergeant you turn reports into who will make these racial jokes."

What the hell? Ty thought. *It's day one, and racial jokes and comments are being discussed by my training officer. Word travels fast, and officers from Hometown PD will talk to their Country PD buddies. Well, let me think the worst but hope for the best.*

"You do not want that sergeant, especially during your training period, pissed at you as a new officer!" Officer Sincere continued. "Some will kick back your report for the smallest mistakes, and there is nothing you can do or say. One final training point: be careful of sergeant shopping."

"You mean, learning which sergeant will be easier on my report?"

"Yes, if they detect you are avoiding one sergeant and going to another, your life on this PD will be rough—there will be hell to pay!"

The next day, Officer Sincere showed Ty around the department. He was introduced to the captain, lieutenant, and several sergeants. Sincere was also an army veteran and felt a kinship to Ty.

"So that is the department chain of command," Ty commented.

"Yes, we are a small agency, and they run the place."

"Who should I watch out for?"

"Let's get through your training so you become familiar with how we police here."

"Cool. Sounds good."

Ty began his short four-week field training and didn't have to deal with any racial jokes or slurs. He was pleasantly surprised and breathed a sigh of relief.

Wow, now I can learn how to be a cop, he thought, relieved.

He finished his training with Officer Sincere and started working as a solo officer.

His experience at Hometown PD was beneficial. Ty's reports improved and weren't kicked back or rejected like they had been at Hometown PD. Six months passed quickly, and everything appeared to be proceeding fine. There were a few racial slurs and jokes but nothing near the level at Hometown PD.

One day Ty walked by the patrol sergeant's office and decided to stop and talk with him.

"Excuse me, sir," Ty began. "I've been thinking about more efficient ways of report writing, which would allow more time for patrol and less time for writing."

"Really?" replied the sergeant, raising an eyebrow. "Six months on the job, and you have suggestions?"

The captain was an old-school my-way-or-the-highway police command officer, which Ty was about to find out.

"Listen, Officer, don't forget your place. I make the rules and policies, not you. Just do your job as a patrol officer and don't worry about changing anything. I'll do my job and make whatever changes when I deem them necessary. Now don't let the door hit you in the ass on the way out. Good day, Officer Washington."

Ty was surprised and quickly realized he had crossed a line. Innovative thinking wasn't the environment at Country PD and probably most police departments in the '80s. Because of this fact, Ty had trouble sleeping that night.

Man, I hope I didn't create another hostile environment by simply wanting to be helpful, he worried.

He started worrying about racial jokes and report rejection. He was just overthinking everything. He reported to a sergeant, not to the captain. It was 1985, and the authoritarian management style definitely ruled the day.

Ty and Diane enjoyed their daughters. One Saturday morning at breakfast, the oldest, seven-year-old Happiness, asked Ty why he was a police officer and not a teacher.

"You see, baby girl, I always wanted to give back to society, to show America Black people can be just as great in serving the country as White people. I am sorry to bring up color to you, but you and your sister see it at school as you have told me. What have I always told you?"

"Daddy, you have taught us that we should always consider who the person is and how they treat us and not let the color of their skin be important."

"Very good, Happiness. You will grow up and be a very responsible woman. Remember, girls, your skin complexion is very light, and some people may not even know you two are Black. You are, and never forget it."

"What about me, Dad?" asked Precious.

"You too, sweetheart. Even at five years old, you are very smart and show how much you care."

"Thank you, Daddy."

"You are welcome, baby girl!"

Ty was experiencing the important lessons of family values, ethics, and love. The role of being a good provider was a social construct, but it was important for the survival of families.

Day in and day out, work seemed to be going well for Tyrone. Two years passed, and except for the occasional racial joke, police work lived up to his dreams. At three years, an experienced Tyrone Washington was performing as a good cop, and his dream was being realized. He felt so good about his lifelong dream.

But he reported to work one afternoon and was informed that Officer Sincere had been fired for misconduct. He called Sincere at home since they had become good friends over the years.

"Man, some chick claimed I made sexual advances on her while I was taking a police report."

"Did you?" asked Ty.

"Come one, man. I am not that stupid because, you know, if a Black man is accused of any misdeed with a White female, game over!"

"Okay, what happened?"

"I was dating her, and one evening she caught me at a restaurant kissing another girl. She became outraged and cussed me out. It was ugly. I left the restaurant with the gal I was having dinner with. The next day, she called the station and filed a complaint against me. She is White, so you know the captain believed her, and I was fired."

"Watch your back, Ty," Officer Sincere warned. "They have kept their racism in check since your arrival. Before you, I was referred to as a 'porch monkey,' 'spear chucker,' et cetera, for years. These assholes have only controlled the racial jokes and comments since you came aboard. With me gone, the racist environment will start once again, and you will be the only target!"

"Thanks for the warning, but things have been good for the past three years, and I may even get promoted."

"Okay, Ty, believe what you want. Just be careful," Sincere insisted. "I will stay in touch with you. Take care, bro."

"You as well, bro."

Sincere was correct. The racial slurs and jokes immediately increased. Sergeant Reliable saw Ty in the hallway and said, "Hey, T, is it true that watermelon is the national food of Black people?"

"Wow, Sarge, where is this coming from?"

"Thought I would spark things up with our one and only Negro."

Ty walked away, thinking, *Is this shit going to start again?*

The racial jokes increased as Jones had said they would. Ty started taking this pressure home.

"Honey, the bullshit racism is increasing at work," he complained to his wife. "Guys I thought were my friends have started the racial slurs and jokes."

"Do not pay attention to them," his wife replied. "You are a good, intelligent man."

"Diane, you just do not understand. Day after day it's racial comment about this, racial comment about that. It was cool for a couple of years."

"You must be strong and not let them get to you. I know it is easy for me to say since the comments are not directed at me."

After a few rough weeks, Ty and Diane had a major argument, and Ty focused more on his two daughters than on his wife.

"You know, Diane, we argue more than a newly married couple with kids should. I know I bring the stress of work home sometimes."

"Yes, you do, but I notice it is directed at me more than the girls, and that is good."

"Listen, you are a good mother, but my frustration at work is not a benefit to you. Maybe we need to be apart," Ty told his wife. "I do not want you and the kids listening to me complain every day."

"I agree. Okay, your anger is increasing, and we are arguing too much in front of the kids."

"Our daughters deserve the best, so I will move out," Ty said. "I think separation is best, but they will never want for anything, and I will be there when either one needs me."

"I hate to agree with you, but as long as you take care and provide for the girls, separation may be best."

Within two weeks they were separated and Ty moved into a one-bedroom apartment. The kids stayed with Diane, and Ty visited his daughters weekly. Ty was sad that he hadn't been able to balance his job and his marriage. After a year of separation, they divorced. He always supported the girls, taking them to various fun places including Disney World and amusement parks.

The divorce weighed heavily on him, and he wanted to make sure his daughters didn't suffer. Since he was a weekend father, there were many outings and various entertainment activities Ty enjoyed with his girls. He emphasized to his girls the importance of education, honesty, and hard work, even though they were only five and seven years old. His religion helped through these difficult times.

While working at Country PD, Ty's mother fell ill to the dreaded disease called cancer. He visited her as often as he could, but the work hours made it difficult.

His father called and said, "Your mom is not doing well. You need to come see her."

Ty drove the 120 miles to his mom's apartment.

"Son, the doctor gave me just a few months," she said. "I have made all the preparations. My greatest wish is that you and your brothers stay close always."

"Don't worry about that, Mom. I will continue to pray for you."

Ty left her apartment, but he didn't know how to cope with the thought of his mother's death, his divorce, and the hostile work climate.

Within two months, Ty's mother ended up in the hospital, fighting the best she could. Ty and his one brother George were in the lobby when the doctor came down the hallway. "I regret to tell you your mom has gone home and is in the presence of God."

Ty called Ronald, and he flew home the next day. Ronald arrived home, and the brothers grieved together and buried their mom. Ty remembered the day his mom was laid to rest. His mother's passing was devastating. She has been his best supporter, mentor, and champion. She had always supported his dream of becoming a police officer. Her words of warning about racism resonated with him on a constant basis. Her voice of advice, comforting words of courage, and motivation would be missed since they laid the foundation of Ty's character.

Looking back at her remarkable life, Ty remembered his mom telling him about her days of living in the Deep South, where she had experienced the "colored only" drinking fountains, bathrooms, and restaurants, eventually fleeing the segregation and bigotry of the South to come to the inner city, setting the stage for Ty to be all he could be. She had shown her love for Ty by demonstrating respect for his profession, but she'd also been direct and honest, cautioning him that he might never really be accepted in his career of choice. Now he had to go it alone, but his mom had built a solid foundation for him. After a few days of grieving, Officer Washington returned to work.

Ty enjoyed being a police officer, especially visiting and talking to kids at schools. He wanted to project a positive image to kids who seemed to distrust police more and more. He began to think and develop opinions regarding policing in the lower-income areas (a.k.a. the ghettos).

One afternoon at the department, Sergeant Reliable asked Ty to step into his office.

"I understand you have ideas regarding policing and the schools in this city. Too bad. Forget them. I'm the boss! But despite your independent attitude about how to police this city, you show promise. I would like to have you work part-time weekly in the detective bureau."

"Thanks, sir. I will work very hard!"

"You'd better work your ass off."

"No problem, sir. You can count on me."

Ty left the office, walked down the hall, exited the back door into the parking lot, and let out a yell. "Yahoo!" he shouted.

Ty reported to Detective Sergeant Brent's office.

"Welcome, Ty," Brent greeted him. "Welcome to the detective bureau. There is a lot of work for you. Here's your caseload of burglaries, robberies, and one homicide. Get to work."

Brent started to walk away, then turned back. "Keep me informed of what you do, Washington. I don't want the lieutenant coming down on me for shit you screw up."

"Will do, Sarge."

After two months of hard work, Ty was assigned full-time into the detective bureau. Detective Washington was successful in police work.

One Tuesday afternoon, Sergeant Brent stopped by Ty's tiny office and said, "Ty, you're doing great. Keep closing cases. It is making the lieutenant happy."

Ty remembered what Officer Sincere had told him, so he asked a fellow officer, "What is a 'porch monkey'?" Sergeant Brent had handed him a cartoon leaflet that depicted a monkey on a porch reading a newspaper. Below the money was a caption. "Porch monkey hard at work."

"It's a joke, Ty," the officer said. "Don't be upset. Humor is important in this job as a detective."

Ty had never heard the term *porch monkey*. After work, he called his friend Lew, and asked him, "What the hell is a 'porch monkey'?"

"It is a demeaning term used to describe Black people. White people believed Black people looked like monkeys, and 'porch monkey' was used to describe those Blacks who were on welfare and sat on the front porch, drinking and talking shit all day."

"We as Black folk do not help with this porch monkey stereotype."

"Ty, who used that term?"

"My sergeant," replied Ty.

"Wow! Why would your sergeant say that?"

"Hey, who knows why people think racial jokes are funny?"

"This the first time I have ever heard a derogatory word from this sergeant, Ty. Go easy. Don't overreact."

"No problem. Thanks."

Ty ignored the porch monkey incident and concentrated on his job. As a detective, he was now responsible for reviewing thousands of police reports patrol officers submitted for investigation. He reviewed each one and prioritized which cases had sufficient evidence to follow up on. Some of the crimes were years old and considered cold, with insufficient evidence to solve them. Those cases had to be closed. Ty was passionate about working narcotics cases. He saw these crimes as the type to physically and mentally impact the health of society.

One of the perks of being a detective that Ty enjoyed was the wearing of plainclothes, a concept Ty thought about as he watched police TV shows. Ty's favorites were *Starsky & Hutch* and *21 Jump Street*. Ty generally wore a shirt and tie with dress slacks. He wore blue jeans only during surveillance or actual search warrant execution. Once a week, he donned a uniform and worked patrol when a shift was generally short of officers because of sickness or vacation. His new badge said "Detective" instead of "Police Officer"—a milestone for Ty's career in policing.

One afternoon in the hallway, Ty overheard the lieutenant talking to Sergeant Brent. "Listen, Sergeant Brent, I told you to make sure these damn reports were on my desk on time."

Brent started to reply, but the lieutenant interrupted, "Get your ass in my office."

"Yes, sir," replied Brent.

After a few minutes Brent walked out and entered the detective office.

What an asshole, thought Ty. *To order a sergeant around like a dog is unconscionable.*

However, the tables turned on Ty. Sergeant Brent walked into Ty's office and said, "What the hell are you doing in the station, Ty? With all these burglaries taking place, get your ass in the streets and arrest some crooks!"

"Hey, Sarge. Just because you got your ass chewed by the lieutenant, there's no need to be getting on me."

"Okay, fine, just get out there and try to close some cases."

Ty left the station and went on patrol in an unmarked police car—yes, just like *Starsky & Hutch*. Being a detective was great; he developed informants, citizens who provided sensitive narcotic information to police, which led to search warrants, arrests, and seizure of drugs. The use of confidential informants is a common police practice and a normal police tool used to solve crimes.

It was Ty's lucky day. He spotted one of his snitches, so he pulled his unmarked car into a side alley, out of public sight, and met his informant Squeaky.

"Squeaky, tell me something good."

"No problem, Ese," Squeaky said. "Chavo is selling some *mota* [marijuana] and some *chiva* [heroin]."

"Sounds good, but do you think we can buy from him?"

"You know, Ese, he's really careful about who he sells to."

"Thanks, man, this better be good info."

"*Ahorale pues*, right on," Squeaky replied.

Ty returned to the station to brief the sergeant on his snitch's info.

"Well, Detective, this sounds like good info, and I know this snitch has provided reliable info in the past," Sergeant Brent replied. "Okay, let's get started. Write the search warrant, and let's put an operation together."

Ty was excited beyond words. Finally, he was going to be a real cop.

He began writing the search warrant in accordance with department policies, the courts, and, of course, the provisions of the US Constitution. There were key facts like where the narcotics in the house were stored, how much, and the type of house (one or two story). Search warrants are very important tools in policing and exemplify the procedural importance of our laws. Experienced detectives demonstrate guidance in writing search warrants according to law enforcement training standards.

Search warrants reflect the importance of following the law as written in the Fourth Amendment of the US Constitution, which prohibits unreasonable searches and seizures. Search warrants provide police with the legal right to enter a home or building to legally search for and seize contraband.

Ty respected the boundaries and limitations of the US Constitution—in this case, the requirements of the Fourth Amendment. The first part of obtaining the approval was writing the affidavit, which was basically an executive summary outline of what was expected to be found and seized in the warrant.

Ty finished writing the warrant, drove to the court, and requested an audience in the judge's chambers. Upon entering the chambers, he handed the judge the warrant, who read the contents.

"Detective, this looks like a well-written warrant," the judge said. He signed the warrant and wished Ty well.

As Ty was returning to his office, he called the narcotics task force office and advised the sergeant that the judge had signed the warrant.

Phase one in this search warrant was surveillance, whereby operational intelligence was collected, analyzed, and utilized. The suspect was Chavo, a local drug dealer, and surveillance was set up on his house. The execution of a search warrant required precision planning and execution, and the narcotics task force drafted an operation plan. This was a great learning process for Ty.

The plan was to conduct a controlled buy whereby the informant was given the buy money and sent to the dealer's home to make a drug purchase. After the purchase, the informant returned to the waiting officers, who were nearby in a concealed location. The law requires the informant be kept under observation—in other words, entering and leaving the house as identified on the warrant.

Ty and the other investigators watched from a distance with binoculars while Squeaky entered the house. While they waited in the alley, a couple of the local schoolkids walked by and recognized Ty from the talks he had given at their school, and the kids had no way of knowing Ty was on a stakeout.

"Hi, Officer Washington, are you undercover or something?" one boy asked.

"As a matter of fact, I am. Please keep moving. I'll talk to you guys later."

Ty turned just in time to see Squeaky walking out of the house. The officers left the stakeout location and met him back at the rally point.

"Here you are, man," Squeaky said, handing Ty a plastic bag full of marijuana.

Squeaky was searched to make sure he hadn't held back a little pinch for himself.

"Where does he keep his stash?" Ty asked about the house.

"In his bedroom and the refrigerator."

"Okay. I'm going to check out your info and get back with you. If it's good, we'll talk to the judge about giving you a break on your pending cases."

"Cool, man. Thanks," Squeaky said as he walked, and now it was time for the team to execute the search warrant.

The next day, the task force met in the conference room at the PD. The task force members were from different police departments in the county. A diagram of the house was drawn on the chalkboard, and the task force detectives were given various assignments in the execution of the search warrant. The operational briefing concluded, and the task force left the PD and convoyed a short distance to the house, where the warrant would be executed.

A uniformed officer knocked on the front door as the rest of the team surrounded the house and concealed their appearance as best as possible. "This is the police department! We have a search warrant for this residence."

They waited approximately twenty seconds, and when no one answered, the uniformed officer attempted to kick the door open. He kicked the door with all his strength, but it didn't budge.

Ty swaggered up to the door and said, "Okay, guys, watch this."

He took two steps and made a flying side leap at the door. *Wham*! He hit it like a rocket and fell to the ground by the impact, but alas, the door still didn't open. The front door entry team laughed within a few moments, and the front door started slowly opening, and out walked Detective Glory.

Ty asked, "How'd you get in?"

"The back door was unlocked, so I just walked in and opened a rear unlocked window without telling the others and crawled into the house."

The dope dealer Chavo wasn't home, so the task force officers began searching the house.

"Hey, Ty, come in here," Detective Glory said. "Feast your eyes on this!"

In the closet, the officers had found foil wrappers of heroin and several large plastic baggies of marijuana. The narcotics were seized, taken to the police station, and booked into evidence.

Sergeant Brent walked into Ty's office and said, "Nice bust. Good work. This should please his honor, our mighty lieutenant."

"I doubt it," Ty said. "That asshole ain't happy with nothin', no matter how much we bust our asses."

After booking the evidence, Ty processed an arrest warrant for Chavo. He turned in his report to Sergeant Morales, and the search warrant raid hit the local media and put the department in a very good public light. Ty and Sergeant Morales later arrested Chavo.

About four months later, Ty wrote another search warrant, walked it to the court, where a judge signed it. Squeaky made another controlled buy; and the task force assembled, reviewed the operation plan, and set out to execute another narcotics search warrant.

The task force arrived at the search warrant location and knocked at the front door. "This is the police department. We have a search warrant for this residence. Open the door!"

Sergeant Consideration and the others didn't wait twenty seconds before the door was kicked open and everyone rushed in. The suspected dealer, Pepe, was sitting on the living room couch; when the officers entered the living room, Pepe ran down the hall toward the bathroom.

Sergeant Consideration and another officer grabbed him and began placing him in a controlled hold.

"Stop, you're breaking my fucking arm!" Pepe yelled.

"Come on, guys, the arms really weren't made to bend like that," Ty said.

They didn't respond; so Ty grabbed Pepe, pulled him away from the officers, and handcuffed him.

"Thanks, man, they were breaking my arms."

"You have the right to remain silent," Ty said and continued advising Pepe of his Miranda rights.

This was another good bust, since several packages of heroin, marijuana, and barbiturate pills were seized.

Ty was on a roll, and now he was living his dream of being a cop. He returned to the station, and the lieutenant unexpectedly greeted him, praising Ty and both sergeants on the drug seizure.

For the moment, Ty's experiences were positive. He still heard the occasional racial jokes, but they didn't interfere with his work. But the jokes were still there. Sergeant Brent liked to tell sexist jokes and the occasional racial joke. Ty didn't like hearing the sexist jokes. He believed if they are telling sexist jokes to him, they were probably telling racist jokes when he wasn't present. He expressed his disapproval of the sexist jokes. Some of the officers often referred to him as "Mr. Sensitive" and a "bleeding-heart liberal."

Besides all the racist and sexist jokes, work was becoming interesting. Ty enjoyed his job, and after a few years, he decided it was time to get back on patrol. He liked to laugh as much as anyone. Jokes were funny, but they shouldn't be racially offensive.

One afternoon, Ty was eating at a nice restaurant in a three-piece suit with his nice, shiny badge and gun under his suit coat.

"Hey, brother man," an unknown male said, who approached Ty while he was eating. "You wanna buy some of this good weed?"

"Sure, man. How much?"

"Eighty bucks for a bag, almost a pound."

"Where is the dope?"

"Here in my car. Check this out."

Ty left his meal and walked with the unknown man outside into the parking lot.

He handed Ty a greenish, rectangular brick-like object; it was tightly wrapped in clear plastic, and Ty handed him the money. As the man started walking away, Ty called out to him. "Excuse me, sir. You're not going to like this, but you are under arrest."

"Bullshit, you ain't no cop. That badge ain't real. There aren't any Black cops in this part of the city!"

"Wrong. Look closely at my badge," Ty said. "Now turn around and grab a piece of the wall."

Ty handcuffed the man, who didn't resist. Ty transported the male subject to jail and booked him for sales of narcotics. Sergeant Easy, the administrative sergeant, later saw Ty walking down the hall and asked him to come into his office.

"I read your report about your dope bust last night. Don't ever arrest any narcotic dealer by yourself. What a stupid rookie mistake from a veteran officer!"

The irony was, the practice seemed to flourish in large agencies. Learning the job can be conflicting for any new officer, yet it seemed to Ty, Black and female cops appeared to have the added burden of racism and/or sexism and their every move scrutinized and evaluated. One of the areas was report writing, the essence of police work and a complex task for new officers. Many believed report writing was "weaponized" and used as a tool to discipline, counsel, or terminate targeted officers. In many situations, the targeted officers were minorities and females.

CHAPTER 7

The Vipers Strike!
Country PD

After two fun and successful years of detective work, Tyrone Washington finished his tour in the detective bureau and rotated back to the uniformed patrol division, which generally meant promotion to sergeant but not for Ty. Instead, he was transferred to another division of the PD. This division was short in personnel, and the department felt it was necessary to transfer Ty, an experienced detective, who was back in uniform.

They generally didn't move an experienced detective into uniform patrol without promoting him, Ty thought. *Maybe I am being groomed for promotion to sergeant? That would be great!*

Another thing was, this new division was known as the roughest division in the department. It was said that if someone survived this division, he or she deserved a promotion, a raise, or a great assignment. Ty was eager to apply his newly acquired experience as a detective.

Ty reported to work, entered the new division's downtown offices, and walked into the watch commander's office. He accidently heard a conversation between two sergeants.

"You know, these Mexicans are so stupid. They keep breaking simple laws because they do not speak our language," one White sergeant said. "They do not speak the king's English. Ha ha! If we shipped their asses back to Mexico, we wouldn't have to work so hard."

"That will never happen," the other White sergeant said. "We are in California, and some liberal legislator will ask for exception to deportation, give them a path to citizenship, or give sanctuary to those illegal immigrants. These wetbacks come into our country illegally and use our welfare and health services."

No way, thought Ty. *Not again!*

"Excuse me, Sergeant. My name is Tyrone Washington. I am reporting for duty."

"Yes, Officer Washington, we have been expecting you. Your training officer will be Officer Ego," the sergeant said as Officer Ego walked into the office.

"Sir, I have been on the department nearly four years," Ty retorted. "I do not require a training officer."

"Yes, but you have been working in the detective bureau and need some refresher training. We do it for everyone."

Ty and his training officer left the station.

"This is bullshit. I do not need a training officer."

"Yeah, policy is policy for this division, and if I were you, I would keep those comments to yourself."

"Thanks for reminding me."

"So, Officer Washington, you were reassigned to patrol because of our shortage of experienced personnel."

"Yes, so what's it like here—dope, burglaries, robberies, or gangbangers?"

"We rock and roll here. This is a armed robbery heaven, because the interstate goes through our city like an inner city. It should be slow tonight. We arrested a bunch of gangsters last week."

The night was slow indeed. The shift ended, and Ty drove home.

Ty finished training in a couple of weeks and once again was a solo officer on patrol. One evening after work, he went to a local restaurant for dinner; and as he walked in, he noticed some of the officers from his new division.

"Look who it is, our token boy," shouted Sergeant Hardass "Hey, Ty, come over and have a beer with us!"

"Sure, Sarge, thanks."

"Hey, Ty, I got a joke for you," one officer began. "What do you get when you mix a Mexican and an Oriental? A car thief that can't drive!"

Several of the officers laughed, but Ty didn't.

"How about this one?" the officer continued. "What does Kinney Shoes have in common with America?"

"Don't know. What?" Ty asked.

"Thirty thousand black loafers!"

Ty thanked them for the beer and left.

Party Invitation

When: June 19, 1984 (Malcom X is up)
Time: 9:00 PM until …
Where: Center Street House (Willy's place)
More class than Poachee's nightclub. Cover charge is a bottle of Thunderbird!

Be there or you Mama! Featuring the world's only Black Virgin.

Featuring: Richard Pryor teaching Boy Scouts how to start a fire with nothing but cocaine, ether, and a BIC lighter! (with background music by the band Freebase!)

Dudes throwing party: Jerome, Marcus, Tyrone

BYOB but Shermes provided.

Bring your own ribs, melons, chitlins, greens, White women. No ghetto blasters allowed under 100 watts per channel.

P.S. Bathe before coming.

During his first week in the new division, the racial slurs started. While on patrol, Ty conducted a bank check and befriended one of the bank tellers, Dawn. After a few weeks, he asked her out to dinner and she accepted. During dinner she asked how he like being a police officer.

"So how long have you been in the police department?" Dawn asked.

"About five years."

"Do you like the job?"

"Yes, it is challenging, but it has its perks."

The conversation moved quickly.

"How long have you been divorced? Do you have children?" asked Dawn.

"Yes, about a year, and I have two beautiful daughters."

After dinner, they watched a movie, and Ty drove her home. There was no kiss the first night but a yes to a second date.

About two weeks later, Ty picked her up, and they went dancing. Disco was the stuff. They danced to the O'Jays, Earth, Wind & Fire, and the Bee Gees. After the club, they went to a late dinner.

"Ty, you are fun to be with," Dawn said. "Tell me about being a cop."

"My lifelong dream was to become a cop, and after many attempts, it finally happened. But I wasn't ready for the sheer volume of racial jokes and slurs. My colleagues tell these jokes frequently, and it creates a hostile working environment. It makes my dream job a nightmare, but I will not quit."

"Ty, I am so sorry. People are just shit and cannot live and let live."

"I have been a cop for seven years, and they have been filled with turmoil, mostly around me being Black in a primarily White, male-dominated profession. Racial jokes and slurs have been the norm, but in this new division thus far, there are fewer racial jokes. I don't understand why White officers act as though they are compelled to tell racial jokes. I dealt with this at my two previous PDs. I transferred to escape the verbal racial persecution, but it never stopped."

"I will always pray for you, Ty. I am sorry for your pain," Dawn empathized. "It is surprising and extremely distasteful to hear about your agony. I understand because as a woman, I experience sexual harassment as well. I understand how important being a police officer is to you. Try to ignore the racist jokesters. Do your job as best you can. We are in the '90s now, and things have to improve."

"Yeah, being Black is a little easier today than in the past but not really, especially in police work."

"Don't let them get to you," Dawn said. "If they see you are upset, they will set a trap to fire you."

"Thanks, Dawn. I truly appreciate your support," Ty affirmed. "It is good to have someone to talk to about this stuff."

After their dinner, he drove her home. "Good night, Dawn. Let's go out again soon."

"Absolutely," she replied.

There were very few Black officers at this division. As the months passed, the racial jokes increased and his police department mailbox contained racist literature.

Ty decided he was no longer going to tolerate the racial slurs and harassment. He fought back by quickly confronting any officer who made a racial slur. He collected the racial leaflets he had received over the past several months. The new toleration strategy was exhausting and pitted him against many officers in his agency, including supervisors. The frustration manifested itself in his work performance. He was doing only enough to get by, with fewer arrests, tickets, and less self-initiated contact. His reports became sloppy, and he was defiant to the sergeants and openly protested report rejections where there were minor mistakes.

Another by-product of Ty's no-tolerance strategy was the mounting racial verbal assault against him. Ty finally snapped, and unleashed his frustration!

He approached Sergeant Bubba, one of his division sergeants.

Bob put out his cigarette, closed the door, and told Ty to have a seat and relax.

"Sarge, I am not concentrating on my job," Ty began. "With all the racial harassment, I cannot focus on it. You already know how my reports suffer from time to time."

"Don't worry. We all make mistakes, but you should have known better. After all, you are an experienced officer and know some of the officers are bigoted assholes. I trust now that you understand the seriousness of your conduct and the recent poor performance, and I will tell you. The division captain is not happy with your performance."

"Yes, sir, I know. How the hell am I supposed to focus with the racial hostility I experience weekly? And when I complain, I am considered thin-skinned and not accepted by my peers."

"Ty, be careful. You are not the favorite son of this administration, and they may discipline you."

"Thanks for listening, Sarge. It is reassuring to see your concern and understanding in this situation."

Ty left the sergeant's office and vowed to himself to change and get back on track.

Two weeks later, the captain called him into his office. "It has been reported to me that your performance is substandard and doesn't conform to department standards. You have been falsifying reports by failing to accurately take down information."

"Sir, I haven't falsified any report. I have written some poor reports and haven't been as enthusiastic as I should. I have been under a great deal of stress from my coworkers. They are constantly telling racial jokes and using offensive language when referring to me or other Blacks."

"We all have our problems, Officer. You're an experienced officer, and there is no excuse for your negligent and incompetent performance. We are conducting an internal investigation into your performance and conduct."

"What? You must be kidding! Why doesn't the department put as much effort into preventing the constant barrage of racial jokes and slurs? This is the conduct that is causing me to be so-called negligent. I am human, sir! I am called these degrading names on a routine basis, and no one seems to care or take action. I am working in a very negative and hostile environment!"

"You watch your mouth, Officer Washington," the lieutenant warned. "I have been told by the sergeants that all you do is make excuses for your poor performance in this division. I do not want to hear anymore. You are dismissed. Get out of my office before I fire you for insubordination here and now!"

Ty departed the Captain's office and couldn't believe the captain's insensitivity and noncaring attitude. He decided to set this encounter aside and focus on doing a good job at this new division.

Ty met Alberto, another cop friend, for lunch, again seeking advice and support.

"I don't understand, Alberto. I just can't think straight," Ty said. "I told Sergeant Bob how I screwed up a case in hopes that he would help me. All I wanted from him was advice. Instead, he runs to the captain, spills his guts, and now I'm under Internal Affairs investigation. I'm looking at some beach days [suspension days]."

"Listen, Ty, we have talked before about your department and the acceptance ritual and the atmosphere of racial disharmony. I heard about your situation through the almighty grapevine. I had a similar situation with my department. I handled a robbery call one day, and I had to shoot the suspect, who was White, after he shot at and hit my patrol unit. Man, you'd think I was the suspect by the way the department investigated the incident! Sometimes I wonder; if the suspect had been Black or Hispanic, would the investigation have been so detailed? The arrogance of the investigators was appalling but understandable since I am Hispanic and the suspect was White.

"The department didn't believe anything I said. Suddenly everything I did turned to shit, and my performance was considered substandard. I confided in one of my sergeants, who told me not to worry and that it would pass. I was later disciplined and suspended for several days. So much for confiding and believing in someone. Hell, Ty, I'm Hispanic, and the department targeted me because I am outspoken.

"Don't misunderstand me. I know it is much worse for you, being Black. Do not trust anyone and keep your thoughts to yourself. Fight the urge to talk and complain to others about your dilemma. None of your fellow officers are your friends. They will throw you under the bus in a second."

"Thank you, my friend. I appreciate your support."

Ty saw the writing on the wall. Once again, it was time to move on to another department. That wasn't good.

Moving again would indicate instability, regardless of the legitimate racial harassment. He had now worked for two police departments—which really was three because of the two divisions in the same department with different people—in less than six years. Could he find another police department that was free of racial harassment?

Ty had three hobbies to relieve the stress and frustration at work. He enjoyed jogging on the beach, golfing, and going to the movie theater. He could give Gene Siskel and Roger Ebert a run for their money in rating movies. He left work one day and went to the movies to relax. The following day, he went jogging at beach. The exercise was for his weight control. Ty had gained about forty pounds since high school and his first military tour. He was realizing that the dream of being a good cop didn't pertain to African Americans—at least, in smaller agencies, not inner city Atlanta or New York.

The sergeant called Ty into the watch commander's office.

"Ty, I regret to inform you that a serious complaint was filed against you by a female citizen. The matter will be investigated thoroughly, and you may need to seek legal representation. Here is a copy of the complaint."

Ty was shocked. "What do mean, Sarge?"

"Ty, do not make any statements. You can leave now."

Ty was perplexed by what they were talking about. He remembered talking with a female salesperson at the local JCPenney while in uniform on duty. He had seen her before and would say hello. One day while talking with her, she told him about an exclusive private nightclub where she worked. Ty asked her whether she could put him on a guest list, allowing him entry. She replied no, asked why he was being so personal, and said that stopping her as she was working was wrong. Ty immediately stopped talking to her and walked away.

After several weeks of waiting, the Internal Affairs (IA) investigation was concluded. Ty was called into the deputy chief's office with the lieutenant present.

"Ty, you're a good cop," the deputy chief spoke. "I know you have had some problems. But the Internal Affairs investigation ordered by the lieutenant showed you being negligent and acting improperly with a female citizen, and you kissed off or didn't take a report from the victim of a theft."

"Excuse me, sir?"

"Instead of doing your job and reporting the theft report, as the female victim asked, you didn't write the report. You told her there was no way we could find any suspects and that writing the report was a waste of time."

"Okay, sir, I do not remember making that statement, but if I did, my experiences would have allowed me to make the determination. There was no suspect information and no physical evidence, so there was nothing to report."

"Officer, you take a report and say there is no suspect information or physical evidence? That is not the worst of it. After not taking the report, you asked her out on a date. On duty. While in uniform!"

"Sir, I merely asked her whether she would like to have coffee sometime, and she said no, and I left it at that."

"Well, this wasn't the same incident at JCPenney, but it was the same female."

Ty suddenly realized he'd screwed up. He hadn't asked her out, but he had asked to be put on the guest list, and somehow she alleged that he'd asked her out on a date.

The Deputy Chief rendered his punishment. "This is conduct unbecoming a police officer, and you are suspended without pay for three weeks."

"You know, sir, that's not fair. Don't I get some sort of representation? Hell, crooks are afforded due process rights, so why not me? Don't I get to defend myself?"

However, unfortunately, the California Peace Officer Bill of Rights was only a few years old, and most department supervisors didn't care.

"You had a chance to join the police officer association and you chose not to, and thus you have no representation. You are hereby suspended for three weeks. Hand me your badge and weapon, and I will see you in three weeks."

A bewildered and angry Ty left the deputy chief's office and wondered, *How could the lieutenant do an impartial investigation on me and then give me such a harsh discipline, three weeks without pay?*

Ty's mistake was that he had dismissed this encounter with the female. She was White and had filed a complaint against him several weeks ago. In addition, he discovered the female was a girlfriend of one of the officers who had been making racial slurs.

All the months of racial harassment and discrimination by fellow officers and supervisors, and now I am suspended for making a dumb comment? Ty pondered. *I can accept a verbal or even a written reprimand but not such a harsh punishment of three weeks off with no pay and a permanent record in my personnel file!*

During his suspension, Ty discussed his situation at Country PD. One of his friends, John, was an attorney. He gave his theory on racism in policing. John was an accomplished, educated man and a Black police captain in another agency.

"Ty, you are entering a new era of racism," John said. "Generally, you will not be called offensive language to your face. Racism is becoming very covert. This new form of racism is often referred to as institutional racism. The discriminatory acts are woven within the very framework of an organization. In other words, a Black or minority is simply told he or she doesn't meet the minimum standards of the organization. Trivial deficiencies are amplified and used to deny you the opportunity to succeed, and the door to professional development and opportunity is closed in your face."

"Sir, that is a lot to take in and analyze, but I see how important what you said is to survival and partial acceptance in policing. Knowing and being aware that it's an unfair internal system will help me battle through the obstacles."

"Just remember, Ty, it is not a fair system," John said. "We weren't meant to be police in this society, but we are here to stay and succeed."

"Thank you, sir. I will keep that in mind."

"Remember, focus on your job as much as possible and try not to react to the racial jokes and slurs so directly. Be careful how you overtly show your discontentment."

"Thank you, sir."

Ty returned from suspension and tried to focus on his job. Things were calm for a few weeks, but the heat started once again. He found another racial leaflet inside his department mailbox.

He looked at the first page and became so upset and angry that he didn't look at the rest of the document until he went home. The leaflet was an examination that listed every known racial stereotype for Blacks and Hispanics. It used slang terms like "poleece," "ribs and wings," "Kool-Aid," "wire-wheeled El Dorado," "All Saints Baptist Church," and so forth. The leaflet was very defamatory, and Ty was humiliated beyond description.

The shift ended, and while sitting at his kitchen table, Ty opened a beer and began reading the document. He called John and asked to meet to show it to him.

"Sir, look at this shit," Ty began. "Will it never stop?" He handed John the paper.

After reviewing it, John said, "You know, when you read this kind of shit and think about the effort to put something like this together, it truly shows the level of a racist mind. Ty, I am not sure what to tell you. If you file a complaint or tell anyone outside your department, they will label you another thin-skinned Black with a chip on his shoulder. I believe many Whites in the future will not believe this happened.

"All I can say to you is, stay the course," John added. "Policing is a good profession. We just need to be tolerant of personality dysfunction by some of the White officers. Ty, do not be discouraged. One day you will reap the benefit of your due diligence and perseverance in law enforcement. I get it. You can't see the light at this point in your career. It will come, I promise you!"

"Again, thank you, sir, for your time."

Tyrone Washington went home and prepared for work the next day as his dream was seemingly disappearing. "Freedom and justice for all" wasn't in his vocabulary. Many of the joke tellers had never served in the military but had the nerve to treat Ty, a military veteran, in such a defamatory manner. Ty wasn't going to give up; he knew there was more to come, and he had to suck it up. He returned to his Christian roots and started reading his Bible, praying, and going to church more frequently.

"I will not allow these negative comments from colleagues, my so-called brothers in blue. God will guide me through the storm."

CHAPTER 8

Black to the Future

Ty was losing faith in his chosen profession of law enforcement. It appeared racial discrimination and harassment were part of the police culture. He wanted to quit, wait to be fired, or ignore everything. He was unsure and wandered for weeks in the wilderness of professional uncertainty.

As one coping approach, Ty started attending the National Organization of Black Law Enforcement Executives meeting held in another county. He enjoyed listening to senior Black law enforcement officers at one-day seminars. This was his second NOBLE conference.

There seemed to be no relief from the stress of being Black in the blue uniform. Stress was created primarily by the constant racial jokes, and there seemed to be different schools of thought in dealing with racial jokes. Some recommended standing up to the slurs and refusing to laugh at them. Others recommended tolerance, laughing to be accepted, and, when the time was right, protesting and filing grievances.

Ty had experienced the attempt to file a complaint approach, but sergeants had told him it was his poor performance that would rule the day, not the merit of his frivolous racial complaints. Ty began researching this systematic hostile racial environment and discovered many Black officers had the same experiences. The difference was Black officers in large agencies, because the numbers were greater, the hostile racial climate was monitored and kept in check. Initially, Ty believed the Black police officers in large police agencies did not suffer the same level of racial trauma as Black officers in smaller agencies, but he was wrong.

This seminar had breakout sessions, where groups of officers within certain career fields, assignments, or promotion met to provide mentoring. In one session, the discussion centered on racial jokes and slurs. Ty had submitted an issue-to-be-discussed note to the Lt. Facilitator, who raised the issue and spoke directly to Ty.

Lieutenant Understanding, a tall Black man, spoke. "Several of us have encountered these racist jokes and slurs. However, in working at large agencies, the jokes are not constant, and there is a support group of other Black officers to coach and mentor those enduring the slurs. You haven't cornered the market on bigotry and racism in policing. Several of us have also experienced racist colleagues and supervisors."

After the breakout sessions, the attendees walked into the main hall to listen to a guest speaker, Deputy Chief Enthusiasm, another Black police executive. Ty saw him and felt hope.

"Promotion and performance evaluations are used as weapons against us, used as excuses to discipline or terminate.

Work through this career obstacle for all minorities in this career field. As minority officers, you must exceed the standard just to meet the standard of acceptance. Once I tested for a lieutenant position, and after passing the written exam, I failed the oral interview. I never gave up and was eventually promoted to lieutenant, then captain, and now a deputy chief. Has anyone here ever noticed that the higher you go up the organizational ladder, the fewer Blacks you see? This is true in large or small police departments. We must change and overcome these obstacles and other status quo discriminators."

Chief Enthusiasm concluded. He received a standing ovation from the audience.

At this point, another executive-level Black female approached the microphone. Assistant Chief Inspiration addressed the audience.

"Most of you know me. I have lived with these negative aspects of our profession for many, many years—race and gender discrimination and humiliation. I promoted during the turbulent '70s and '80s. I remember seeing segregation when Black officers were only allowed to patrol the Black neighborhoods and discouraged from arresting Whites. Change is in the air. Minority officers will be promoted in greater numbers. This is the future in policing!

"We must learn to do what Whites have been doing for decades in corporate America—coaching, mentoring, supporting others to promote. Remember, it was called the 'good-ole boy' system. Those of us in command staff positions need to act as a ready resource and reference point for young Blacks coming up the ladder. Blacks who are promoted to senior command–level positions must reach out to support young Blacks coming up the ladder. I don't mean favoritism or special privileges but simply afford the opportunity for advancement and offer resource counseling and mentoring. This is the intent of affirmative action, and hopefully, it will last long enough to enhance the upward mobility for minorities."

She concluded and also received a standing ovation. Another speaker came to the podium.

Commander Future walked to the microphone. "Ladies and gentlemen, I must caution you—be careful how you portray yourself at your agencies. You have all heard about the inadequacies within our profession. Do not discuss your racial feelings with any of your fellow White officers, unless you are a blood brother to them or know them exceedingly well. Otherwise, be prepared for retaliation and increased harassment. Listen to me. I have been there! I know!

"To challenge or protest the racial jokes may subject you to discipline by scrutinizing everything you do. You will become a project of those harassing you. This includes receiving substandard performance evaluations. Seek experienced mentors—there are several of us here at this seminar.

"We are out here, and we enjoy coaching and mentoring Blacks coming up the promotional ladder.

"Now if you are the only Black in an agency, it is tough to withstand the onslaught of racial jokes and slurs. Still seek the support. Just understand you are on the professional tree limb and in some cases alone. It may not change the course of the harassment, but it may provide some relief."

The seminar concluded, and Ty contacted one of the speakers.

"Sir, I was motivated by your seminar. I have unwittingly violated those simple rules of conduct that you mentioned earlier. I have voiced my opinion in opposition to the racial slurs. I am the only Black patrol officer in the department. Is there any way I can counteract being targeted for poor performance evaluations, unfair discipline, or termination?"

"All you can do at this point is to really keep a low profile. I assume report writing, poor performance evaluations, and poor attitude are being used against you?"

"Yes, sir, that is very true."

"Hang in there and continue to work hard," the speaker said. "Ignore the negative and excel as much as possible in the positive. It is not an easy struggle, but we are used to that."

"Thank you, sir."

The attendees exchanged business cards. Many agreed to stay in touch and support each other.

An energized Ty returned to work after this short two-day mental sabbatical. He reported to roll call, checked out his patrol car, and started his patrol duties in beat two. There were no racial jokes, slurs, or leaflets in his mailbox on this first day back.

Ty received a radio call at about eleven thirty p.m. about a disturbance in progress at the Pizza Tavern. He responded to the location, and as Ty pulled into the driveway, one of the waitresses approached his police car. He rolled down the window, and from a few feet away, she started talking. "There's a bunch of nig—eh, some people inside creating a disturbance." She'd changed the word as she came closer to the police car and saw Ty.

"No problem, miss. I'll handle the problem."

Ty walked into the tavern, saw the black youths, and advised them to be cool and not to create a disturbance but to enjoy the victory celebration of their college football team. Ty returned to his patrol car and resumed his patrol duties.

This was one of the few incidents when Ty heard a negative racial slur from a community member. It was interesting to him because it was nighttime, he was Black, and the waitress couldn't see him clearly in the police car.

I've been going about things all wrong, he thought. Complaining and filing a grievance may not be the answer. I can't let my emotions get in the way of logic and reason. I will work hard and overcome organizational anxiety.

Ty ended his shift and returned to the station. As he passed the police department mailbox, he saw another leaflet inside. He removed it; it said, "Rats, burned another one." The leaflet was distasteful; it depicted a picture of God or Jesus making this comment.

He went home and talked with Dawn. "It never stops. I have no idea who put this leaflet in my locker, but I can guess. It is probably the same ones who make the racial jokes.

"It's funny, Dawn. The same officers who make the racial slurs are often accused of using excessive force," Ty voiced his opinion. "These officers cover for each other when they violate policy. I put up with racial intolerance, which appears to violate my civil rights."

"Ty, is this truly the profession for you? You are bright and educated, and yet you are treated so badly by your fellow officers. You are bigger than this. Quit and use your education in other ways!"

"Yeah, you are right, but I must stay the course," Ty said. "It will get better someday. Sergeant Boldness had put his foot in the back of a sixteen-year-old high school girl because she called him a stupid asshole. Sergeant Do-Right smacked a fifteen-year-old high school kid in the head with the butt of his gun simply because the kid was ditching school and had made the mistake of running from him. And when he caught the kid, he said, 'Don't ever run from me, you little fucking beaner.' Someone has to hold them accountable."

"True but not the one who is always receiving derogatory racial slurs and being discredited by the bosses. You have to be in a position to make a difference," Dawn advised.

Do-Right ordered Ty to take the kid to the hospital for treatment. The kid's face was a red mess, blood dripping everywhere. While waiting for the kid to be treated, the nurse asked the kid, "What happened to you?"

"A cop hit me in the head with his gun."

"Why?" asked the nurse.

"I ran from him because I was scared," the kid responded.

The nurse looked at Ty, and the kid quickly said, "It wasn't this officer. This officer has been pretty cool to me. It was another cop."

Another good example of wanting acceptance was when Sergeant Do-Right walked past a subject with a gun because it was a White man. When Ty arrived, he noticed something strange about the man; Ty had a hunch and confronted the man. The man was drunk and became belligerent; Ty searched him and discovered the gun. Subsequently he arrested the man. In Ty's mind, if the man had been Black, it would have been a different scene.

"Hey, Do-Right, look!" Ty showed him the gun. "You walked right past the old guy. It's lucky he didn't blow your head off." Ty walked away, thinking it was funny and not realizing he had just embarrassed Do-Right and punctured a hole in his ego. This incident would later cost Ty.

Two days later, when Ty came to work, Do-Right confronted him; he had been the shift supervisor that night. "Here are a few of your reports. Redo them. They are sloppy, and your *T*s and *W*s are not written properly."

"What do you get out of screwing me over like this?" replied Ty.

"I'll tell you. I didn't really like the fact that you were hired over a more qualified White guy. Now it's payback. We'll show you how we deal with affirmative action!"

"Hey, Do-Right, don't bother pulling the knife out of my back. I'll do it for you." Ty left the office and went on patrol.

Two days later, Ty was called into the division commander's office, unsure what was going to happen.

"I have reviewed your performance evaluation, and it is filled with deficient work performance and poor attitude comments by your shift supervisors," the commander said to Ty. "Based on what I have reviewed, it is my decision to terminate you for below-standard performance and the inability to work with your peers."

"What do you mean? Are you aware of the countless racial slurs, jokes, and racist leaflet attacks I have experienced for months?"

"Yes, I've heard the rumors, but no formal complaint was every submitted, and it wouldn't have a bearing on your poor performance."

"No, sir, I haven't formally complained because it is my word against other officers and supervisors. I have verbally expressed my displeasure about the hostile working atmosphere because of the racial slurs and jokes to the sergeants. No one seemed to care or take action. It is clear these officers conspired to get rid of me with supervisors and agreed to write negative and false reports about my performance. What about a hearing, my due-process protection, representation, and innocent until proven guilty?"

"Well, Ty, in case you weren't told, your transfer to this division placed you back on probation, and as a probationary officer, you are not entitled to any representation or other due-process protections. You didn't complete the probation period and are hereby terminated."

"That is wrong and grossly unfair. I plan on getting an attorney to sue for the racial discrimination against me in this division."

"Just turn in your badge and gun."

Ty stood up, handed the commander his badge and gun, and walked out of the office. He left this division, never to return.

He went home and broke the news to Dawn. "Well, sweetheart, it happened," he began. "Those racist assholes finally got to the commander in chief, and I was fired."

"What are you going to do?"

"I will take a short tour in the army. In the meantime, I will take any job I can. Tyrone Washington, the cop who was conflicted with his career, is now a private citizen, stripped of his pride, dignity, and badge."

Ty went to his favorite beach, sat in the sand, and began to pray. He looked over at the sunset and thought about why he wanted to be a cop and that systemic racism wasn't going to stop.

"Dear Lord, be with me. Give me strength, and if it be your will, help me get back into policing. Thy will be done."

Ty shared some thoughts with Dawn. "You know, honey, no one seems to understand but other Black cops, and they are an excellent source of therapy. The old expression 'Birds of the same feather flock together' became a survival tool in police work, but it didn't stop the institutional racism."

"Are you sure you want this for your life and the kids?"

"Yes, it is an honorable profession. I just have to break into the line-up and gain acceptance. I believe I can accomplish this by keeping a low profile and continue seeking mentoring from other Black officers and organizations like the National Organization of Black Law Enforcement Executives (NOBLE). The Hispanic officers have a similar organization. I have friends who are members. I will seek their mentoring and support."

CHAPTER 9

Army Green and Self-Esteem

The unprofessional attitudes, humiliation, and racial harassment were intolerable and so much a part of the 1980s. The sheer volume of racism appeared to be very institutionalized and woven within the very fabric of policing. Ty was another casualty of bigotry and racism in America. Now, as an unemployed cop, he looked for any work he could find.

Wow, I get fired for poor performance, not misconduct or malfeasance, Ty thought. *How is this possible when other officers were disciplined for the use of excessive force, where some were killed or seriously injured? Those officers were found to be within policy, and of course, they were all White officers. It is truly my hope that the future will allow truth, justice, and fairness in the policing system.*

He was able to find a job and worked as a janitor for a large church for a couple of months while he waited to reenter the army.

"You know, Mr. Washington, somehow you don't strike me as a janitor," Ty's supervisor, Sarah, said to him as he was mopping the office floor one Friday afternoon. "Something just isn't right."

"Well, ma'am, I was a police officer who didn't play ball with the boys," Ty replied. "I just didn't fit in. I was the first Black officer of the department. I dealt with racial jokes and slurs during my early years in policing. I couldn't focus on learning my job as a cop. Rather, I worried about where the next racial slur was coming from."

"You know, I remember reading about you in the paper a few years ago when you were hired. You demonstrate a good and positive work ethic, and we enjoy you here. I understand, as a female, that I have to prove myself constantly. Do yourself a favor before you go crazy. Find a way back into police work. It is your calling. Do not let them win. I can see your potential for success!"

"Thank you, Sarah, for the inspiration."

At that moment, Ty heard a siren. He looked out the fifth-floor window and saw a police car going code three, red lights and siren blasting.

Ty lowered his head, then suddenly raised it high and said, "I will return to my dream!"

The janitor job wasn't enough to support his family, so Ty went to the unemployment office. The bills were piling up very quickly, and the creditors were calling weekly. While standing in the unemployment line, he noticed all types of people from all races. Everyone had the same goal— to provide for his or her family—and the unemployment check was a great help to many. He felt very much like the many Americans who were victims of poverty, and some would never be able to climb out of the economic hole. Ty felt ashamed and sorry for the many people he saw at the unemployment office, primarily because he knew someday he would return to prominence in policing and never return to this.

Ty saw a man in the line next to him, who was staring at Ty as if he knew him. After looking at the guy for a while, he remembered. In his last week before being fired, Ty had written a citation to the man for running a stop sign. The guy stood out in Ty's mind because he had said, "The only reason you are writing me a ticket is because you have a badge and gun." The guy was White and didn't make any racial comments.

"You remember me, don't you?" Ty said as he approached the man. "I wrote you that ticket to protect you and your family. You ran the red light and were almost hit by another car."

"Thank you for coming up to me," the gentleman said. "I saw you in line and felt bad because a week earlier, you were receiving a cop's salary, and today you are just like me here in this unemployment office. We are both here to support our families. Thank you, Officer."

Ty shook the man's hand and sat down in the waiting room. Tears started coming to his eyes when suddenly a voice rang out, "Next in line, please walk up to the window."

Ty was handed some unemployment forms. He completed the forms, returned to the line, and handed them to the clerk. A depressed Ty departed the unemployment office.

After his visit to the unemployment office, he went home and watched TV and the political fires of the day. He noticed how politicians spoke on TV. They never seemed to answer a question directly. Rather, they said things so people could draw an inference from their words.

Finally, the day arrived, and he rejoined the US Army. The army provided Ty and his family a good benefit package and gave him time to reflect and heal from the wounds of racial humiliation. The army provided a positive climate and professional healing with no racial jokes, slurs, or leaflets. Before departing out of state for a new military assignment, he discussed his future plans with Dawn.

"I will return to police work," Ty said. "But for now, I am returning to the one positive profession I know—the United States Army."

He departed for Fort Benning, Georgia, to attend the army's Officer Candidate School (OCS). The curriculum consisted of military history, law, strategy, tactics, and philosophy. The physical challenges were ever present in army training. Since he was in good physical shape, Ty attended jump school and became airborne. He was maturing and becoming a leader. The effects of racial harassment from the police department were fading away.

Ty completed Officer Candidate School and was commissioned as a second lieutenant in the US Army. He returned to California and joined an army reserve unit. Ty was a leader and given the authority to command soldiers. He took this responsibility seriously and vowed to treat everyone fairly but also to hold soldiers accountable to the standards and ethics of the US Army.

Ty returned to college and studied very diligently for his bachelor of science degree in criminal justice. He worked as a full-time army reserve officer and was also a full-time college student.

During this reconstruction period in Ty's life, US Army captain Tyrone Washington was mobilized and called into active federal duty in support of Operation Desert Shield and Desert Storm. He went to war—what an experience.

Ty and his military police company boarded a military aircraft and flew from California to Dhahran, Saudi Arabia. The twenty-eight-hour flight was long, with air tankers refueling their aircraft over the Atlantic Ocean. Most of the soldiers slept, Ty included. They were suddenly awakened over Egypt.

"Hey, look out of the window," one soldier said.

Those who were awake looked and saw the famous pyramids. Shortly after seeing the pyramids, they entered Saudi Arabian airspace, and another sight was observed. Two American F-16 fighters were escorting an Air Force C-141 Starlifter aircraft to the American air base in Dhahran, Saudi Arabia.

Ty and his company landed and were immediately deployed to the barracks in nearby Damam. Khobar Towers was rented to the US military for housing. It was a nice facility with marble floors and other nice amenities— definitely not the typical living quarters for US soldiers.

From Khobar Towers, Ty and his company deployed north to Camp Doha in Kuwait City. A few miles from Camp Doha was the infamous "Highway of Death." This was a highway from Kuwait City to the northern Arabian Peninsula and the direct route to Iraq. Saddam Hussein had used this road to travel to Kuwait from Iraq in a blitzkrieg—a sudden and overwhelming military attack. Ty visited the aftermath of the Iraqi retreat from Kuwait. Army helicopter gunships and Air Force A-10 Thunderbolts had hit the Iraqi convoy as it fled Kuwait when the American forces arrived in Kuwait City.

Saddam Hussein had ordered the setting of oil wells in Kuwait on fire as a part of his scorched-earth policy. The famous Texas oil rig fighter Paul Neal "Red" Adair took part in extinguishing some of the oil fires. The Kuwaiti oil fields were among the most plentiful in the world, which many speculate was why Hussein invaded Kuwait. Desert Storm was a short hundred-day war to defeat the Iraqi Army.

In the final days before Ty returned to the United States, he had a strange encounter. He returned for some rest and relaxation in Dhahran, and upon returning to Kuwait, he stopped in a little store for snacks. The clerk at the store greeted him as he was buying his snacks. Ty was in his full-combat gear—helmet, weapon, and camouflage uniform.

"I am Habib. Thank you and America for being here to protect our people."

Habib spoke good English, which surprised Ty. "Thanks, Habib, I appreciate hearing that."

"Don't worry. You will be safe as you travel north back into Kuwait."

"Thank you, Habib."

He walked out of the store, feeling pretty good, and his unit returned to Kuwait and was next deployed to the Iraqi–Kuwaiti border, with the oil fires still burning. Ty couldn't wait to stop by the store and thank Habib and tell him the short mission to the border had been successful.

Ty returned to the store, saw a different clerk there, and asked for Habib. "Excuse me. You speak English?"

"Yes, I do. How can I help you?"

"I stopped by here a few days ago and spoke with Habib and just wanted to speak to him."

"I do not understand what you mean. No one by that name works at this store. I am the owner. Are you sure it was this store?"

"Yes, it is the only one on this road for miles."

"You are correct, one hundred miles, but no one by that name works here or has ever worked here. This is my store."

A bewildered Ty bought a soda and left the store. He would reflect on this incident for years to come.

When Desert Storm ended, Ty and many other military soldiers prepared for departure to the United States. Ty and his unit were happy because everyone who deployed to the combat zone came back alive. The soldiers packed their gear, backpacks, weapons, supplies, tents, and vehicles; then they transported everything to the port in Damam. The next few days were spent loading the cargo ships with the equipment, and after several days of loading, the task was complete. The unit returned to Khobar Towers and awaited the return flight to the United States.

One of the soldiers, Captain Hunt, volunteered to return home on the cargo ship with the unit's equipment. The trip would take about thirty days. Ty asked him why, and his answer was "to decompress and relax."

"I wish you the best. See you in a month!" Ty said, and he and the rest of the military unit flew home about a week later.

They flew into the Philadelphia airport, and Ty remembered hearing the song by Lee Greenwood with the lyrics "I'm proud to be an American where it least I know I'm free." There was a crowd of people who clapped for soldiers as they walked through the airport. This was an extremely humbling experience, one he would always cherish.

On the long flight home, Ty thought long and hard about whether he was going to return to police work. The army was a great career, and he never had the racial encounters that filled his police career.

Tyrone transferred airplanes and flew back home with his military unit. Another large crowd greeted the returning soldiers at the airport. The crowd waved American flags, and a band played music as they deplaned and walked into the airport terminal. The families of the soldiers patiently waited in the terminal.

As he entered the terminal, he saw the large crowds everywhere and started looking for his daughters. After a few minutes, he spotted them. He shouted their names, and they ran to him. "Hey, girls!" He hugged them both.

Ty greeted Diane, now his ex-wife, who had brought the girls to the airport to see their father return home.

"Let's go home!" Ty said.

It was a tough situation for Ty, being divorced and away from his two kids, but he always supported them spiritually and financially. Ty loved and cared for those two girls despite not living with them. He remained a good father to his girls.

Ty didn't return to policing for several years. His dream was shattered by the trend of systematic racism in policing. However, as his mother and cousin had taught him, "Do not let the system beat you. You are a very young, intelligent Black man. Someday you will be the example to all of America that we as Black people will contribute to the success of America!"

CHAPTER 10

Reaching the Mountaintop?
Farmland Police Department

Ty continued his active military service and received a great salary and benefits for the family. He began planning his return-to-policing strategy; first stop was college. He also used the time to provide guidance and direction to his daughters by visiting them weekly and emphasizing the importance of school.

Ty's military life was very productive. He developed great friendships, White and Black. Ty routinely played basketball and golfed with a couple of his close army buddies, Mutt and Jeff. Ty often discussed with Mutt and Jeff what had happened in his early policing days.

The midnineties were a time for sociopolitical change in America, especially for civil rights and policing. President Clinton openly supported civil rights, so much so that he was often referred to as the "first" Black president in America (pre-Obama).

Ty began golfing with his friends and enjoyed the fellowship. During one of those days, they were in the clubhouse, drinking a cold beer. Ty discussed his strategy in returning to police work and one friend, Jeff commented. "You cannot let those racist assholes deter you from what you love. Your heart is in policing."

"Yes, do what you want to do," stated Mutt.

"Yeah," responded Ty. "The army has also treated me fairly because of people like you two, and I have reservations about returning to policing."

"Listen, things have changed substantially over the last few years. There are laws on the books to protect citizens against racial or sexist injustices. You are a damn good army officer. You must return to the profession you really love and be the best cop you can be."

"You are both correct. I will start preparing," Ty said, determined.

"I was a cop years ago, but it didn't work for me," Jeff stated. "So, I joined the army and have never looked back. Police work wasn't for me, and I knew it."

"Listen, Ty, even though I'm White, I have seen the kind of crap you are talking about. You cannot let them win!" Mutt began. "Take some time to readjust your approach and analyze your strategies, as the army has taught you. I emphasize: things are changing, and the overt racial crap of the eighties is disappearing. Forget the past and all the negative, racist comments."

"You are both good friends, and I thank you both."

They ended the day at the golf course, and Ty scored an 86—his very best.

The bond with Mutt and Jeff was an important bonding experience for Ty. This was significant to him because both were White, and race was never an issue. They were true friends and military brothers for life. Mutt and Jeff mentored Jeff in a positive, nonracial manner; again, they never demonstrated the White privilege that seemed to exist throughout America. Ty remembered going to dinner with Mutt and Jeff on a Sunday evening after military staff meeting.

"So, Ty, are you going to try to return to police work? After the way you were treated by those racist idiots at your two police agencies, I wouldn't blame you. Stay in the army and finish it as your new career."

"You are right, but I want to help other Blacks, Hispanics, and females who have the same dream as me," Ty said. "Being a police officer, protecting the innocent or victims of crime, is a noble profession. Yes, the badge and legal possession of a gun are powerful and a compelling position. People seem to look up to police officers, even Black ones!"

"I hear you, but your words and emotions really show your distaste for your dream job," Mutt commented. "I believe in you and don't want you to be demeaned again. Stay in the army."

"Thank you, but I am determined to make a difference. I will return to college, go to law school, and obtain graduate degrees. I will make sure my reports are exemplary and go to the top of the police profession."

They finished dinner, and Ty went home. For the next few days, he analyzed what had been said.

Ty increased the number of college courses, and after several months of active army reserve duty, he volunteered for a short active-duty tour, thanks to Mutt and Jeff. As a newly promoted major in the US Army, Ty felt very confident, and his self-esteem was in full force. He was a true American patriot, and the army filled a void policing didn't.

In less than two years, Ty completed his bachelor's degree and was thinking about going to law school. He was very motivated after this army tour. The army had trained him on how to be a leader through the Officer Candidate School and Military Police Corps Officer Advanced Course. He had received months of comprehensive leadership and management training in the army's many leadership schools. His work ethic, beliefs, and knowledge provided him with a new wealth of experiences. His first assignment was as company commander, responsible for a combat support unit, where he was the executive leader of two hundred soldiers. As commander, he was responsible for personnel actions, promotions, assignments, and million-dollar budgets.

The unit's mission was to provide maintenance deployment support to military transportation assets deploying to war zones. After two years in command, he was reassigned to Fort Bliss, Texas, and reported to a military police unit, specifically the Provost Marshal Office (military police chief) as the new deputy provost marshal, where he worked alongside another military police major. Ty enjoyed this assignment, where he performed military law enforcement functions and managed the various programs—in other words, the military version of community-oriented policing—most importantly, free of racial harassment of any kind.

Ty really enjoyed his military assignments because they were free of overt racial slurs and jokes and therefore a positive work environment. He wasn't naive; discrimination occurred in the military. It was just on a much lower scale, and the focus was on the actual military missions of the soldiers, not on their pigmentation, but that was another story. Ty's education, training, and experiences combined to motivate and push him to success. In addition to this successful military career, he began teaching part-time at the local university.

Ty met Lorraine, a young lady at the university—a sharp, articulate, and beautiful woman. Since his divorce, his daughters had grown into two beautiful young ladies; he felt free to explore a new possible relationship. Lorraine and Ty started dating, and Ty shared some of his past police experiences with her.

Like Mutt and Jeff, she believed Ty should return to his childhood dream profession of policing. Ty continued to encourage his daughters to attend college throughout their lives. A few years of dating passed, and Ty married Lorraine; he prayed his second marriage would last longer than his first one.

In the Christian faith, it is said that when God opens a door, you simply need to recognize it and step through. Ty now had a bachelor's degree in criminal justice and decided he would try to make a major career leap by applying for a police chief position in a small city. A police chief position opened in a small, rural city, and Ty applied.

Ty was attempting a major shift in career direction. He wanted to jump from line-level police officer to police chief. He believed his three years of recent active duty at the ranks of captain and major and supervising more than two hundred soldiers looked very good. Also, he had graduated from two major military executive leadership schools. In total, he had fourteen years of military service (reserve and active), a bachelor's degree, and fourteen years of police experience.

Ty began taking written examinations for police chief in rural communities. After a few weeks, he tested through to the final interviews. There were different interview panels, community panels, professional panels, and city administrator panels.

The first panel consisted of community members, and several questions were asked of him:

"So why should we pick you as chief?"

"I have prepared by learning about this community, the needs, people, and your schools. I want to be a role model in this community and demonstrate a true community policing philosophy."

"What qualities and experience do you bring to this community, and how have you prepared for this interview?"

"I have finished my bachelor's degree and am working on my master's in public administration. I am an army veteran who served in Operation Desert Storm. I attended middle-management supervisor training courses."

Ty finished with this first community panel, and the next one was the professional panel.

"You have no police chief experience. How can you become chief?"

"My extensive military management experience, my living in the inner city and being exposed to crime, and my educational skills will enable me to manage the agency. I am very personable and will interact with the schools, businesses, and residents."

"What is the purpose of city council, and how does it manage city government organizations?"

"The council is responsible for setting policy and enforcing city mission business. The city manager has the day-to-day responsibility to ensure the council's policy is followed. Listening to residents, employees, and business merchants is an important aspect of city council."

The final panel was composed of city administrators—generally, the city manager or assistant city manager.

"What is your understanding of the city's chain of command?"

"Department directors or heads report to the city manager. The city manager is the direct voice to the council and should never be surprised by any department director."

"Should the police chief have direct access to the council without the city manager's approval?"

"I believe the city manager should always be kept informed and not deal with council members without telling the manager. Council members are policy makers, not managers. This is a delicate process and must be handled with care. Police chiefs should be politically astute, not politically involved."

The interview and day-long process concluded.

Ty drove home, thinking, *Wow, after everything that happened at Hometown and Country PDs, I might become a police chief!*

Ty had endured untold hardships, indignation, and racial discrimination for years in policing, and now a new adventure was about to open. Maybe that was the dream he was meant to achieve. Was his life about to change?

Ty went home and watched his old *Starsky & Hutch* and *Miami Vice* shows. He called his friend Bay, whom he hadn't talked with for quite a while.

"Bay, I have been testing for police chief," Ty started. "Can you believe it?"

"Ty, I knew you had the potential, but with all the racial hostility you have lived with, I didn't think you would stay in police work."

"I hear you, but I should hear from them in a few days."

Ty received a phone call. "Mr. Washington, this is the city manager, Bob. Can you come to my office today at two p.m. to discuss the police chief position?"

"Yes, sir, I will be there."

He arrived and walked into the city manager's office.

"Mr. Washington, the city council authorized me to offer you the position of chief of police."

"Sir, that is great. I accept."

"Fine," the city manager said, shook his hand, and directed him to Human Resources to complete the paperwork.

A jubilant Ty left city hall and drove home.

Tyrone Washington, chief of police! he thought.

Ty became the first Black chief of police for the Farmland Police Department, a a small rural community. It was the midnineties, and Ty wanted to promote a new community policing direction. His objective was to provide leadership, mentoring, and a professional direction for the officers in his department.

In preparation for his new role, Ty enrolled in a law enforcement management course with a curriculum of management styles, police operational strategies, and personnel matters. This was the first of many executive management courses. He drove to the Conference and checked into the Marriott hotel. Class started the next day.

The first day of class was interesting for Ty. The instructor, another man named Bob, was a retired police chief, who stressed the importance of leading by example and understanding the people who worked for them.

"Remember, twenty percent of your time will be spent on five percent of the people, and they will substantially impact the organizational climate of the entire department," the instructor began.

Ty raised his hand.

"What about spending eighty percent of your time on the department and delegating the handling of the twenty percent to your subordinate leaders such as the captains or lieutenants?"

"Good point, except part of the twenty percent may be your sergeants, lieutenants, or captains. As the chief, you must become directly involved with the twenty percent because those are the ones who will stab you in the political back by going to your boss, the city manager—or, worse, the city council members. This can create chaos and organizational conflict and hamper your ability to successfully manage the department.

"The first order of business for new chiefs is to assess your organization, learn your personnel, and review the policies and general orders manual. This is a critical yet time-consuming task. Generally, the assessment process can take sixty to ninety days. During this time, it's important to meet and greet every council member. The most important rule for every police chief is to keep your city manager informed—no surprises to the city manager about incidents or events that have occurred. You do not want the city manager to learn about significant police events on the evening news!"

Ty noticed he was the only African American police chief in the thirty-person class, which represented police chiefs from across the state. He interacted well with his classmates, especially Jerry, Ed, and Chuck. The four chiefs became friends during the course, and they attended many training sessions together.

"So, Jerry, what do you think about the concept of focusing so much time on just a few of the employees?" asked Ty.

"I've noticed this is true, and it bothers me. Fortunately, my agency has enough senior supervisors to provide me direct input and status of these trouble employees. I believe in treating everyone fairly, but standards must be complied with."

"I agree," said Ty. "After fourteen years in police work, I have noticed most of management's time is spent on the minority of personnel, which is unfair to most good employees. I guess the squeaky wheel is oiled."

The next day, the instructor, Jose, discussed Internal Affairs investigations. IAs are those investigations ordered when a police officer is accused of misconduct.

"This topic is another one of those important functions requiring careful monitoring by police chiefs. The implementation of due process protects police officers, which makes terminating them a very complex process. The legal protections include representation by an attorney or other competent labor representative. It is a comprehensive fact-finding investigation. Even if an officer is arrogant, disrespectful, or acts in a disdainful manner, he or she is entitled to due-process protection."

This statement hit a nerve with Ty.

"Really?" he asked Jose. "So, mistreatment by employees is tolerated, and supervisors must follow the proper procedures of conduct?"

He couldn't help but think back on the harassment he had endured at the hands of racist police officers, which was sanctioned by supervisors.

"I'm not naive," Jose responded. "I understand many supervisors mistreat employees and get away with it. Specifically, I have seen this with minority and female officers. I don't agree with it, but it happens."

"Yeah, I experienced quite a bit of racial harassment as I was coming up the ranks, but it didn't seem to matter to my supervisors. I was always told to just accept the racial jokes, and acceptance will follow. I was never accepted."

"Unfortunately, old habits die hard, and some of those types of prejudicial attitudes will be slow to change. Racial sensitivity is one of those areas that has long been a source of conflict in policing."

Bob changed topics, and the topic of race was never again mentioned in the class. Ty completed the management course and reported to work at the new PD.

He was very careful and overly cautious in his demeanor and words. Ty was extremely honored to be a police chief, let alone the first Black chief to do so in the city's history. The weight of history was on his shoulders—how would he be reviewed?

On his first day, Ty reported to the city manager's office and introduced himself to the secretary. "Morning. I am Tyrone Washington, the new police chief."

"Morning, Chief, we've been expecting you. I'm Elizabeth, the city manager's secretary. Right this way. He is expecting you."

Ty entered the city manager's office. "Morning, sir. Good to see you again."

"Morning, Chief. Please have a seat."

"Thank you."

Ty and the city manager talked for about an hour, discussing city government, managerial styles, city council, community, and the police employees in general. After their initial discussion, the city manager walked with Ty to the police department next door.

"Once again, I want to congratulate you on the selection as police chief."

"Thank you, sir, I am looking forward to doing the best I can."

After they entered the department, the two department administrators, Captains Abel and Francisco, greeted them. The city manager introduced Ty to both captains and left the police department. The captains walked Ty to his new office, where the sign on the door said "Chief of Police." Ty was excited and humbled at the same moment when he sat down at his desk.

"Welcome, sir. Nice to meet you," Captain Abel stated. "We look forward to a successful organization."

"Thank you very much."

Captain Francisco explained his duties as police commander of operations, responsible for patrol operations.

Captain Abel explained his duties as support services commander, responsible for investigations, dispatch, and jail operations.

"So, Chief, where are you from, and where have you worked?"

"I am from the inner city area and have worked for three police departments, including this one."

Everyone talked about backgrounds and hobbies. This initial meeting was the icebreaker and was very informal. The captains were introducing themselves to Ty and vice versa. Ty's secretary walked into his office and introduced herself. "Sir, I am Anna, your executive secretary."

"Nice to meet you, Anna. Let's discuss my philosophy of management and work distribution."

"Of course, sir."

The captains departed and returned to their offices.

"Chief, let me walk you through the department so you can meet some of the employees."

"Sounds great. Thank you."

After the tour, he returned to his office, and Anna helped him set up his computer and bookshelves. Ty concluded his first day, and it was exhausting. He went home and fell asleep.

He was up bright and early the next day and arrived at his office at seven thirty a.m., preparing to meet the captains at eight a.m. to discuss department operations. Anna greeted him, and Ty discussed his expectations with her and her work ethics. He asked her whether she needed any other supplies, but she did not. Before he knew it, eight a.m. arrived. As the captains sat in his office, he watched the body language as each captain postured by throwing out various topics to see how Ty would react.

"Morning, Chief. What are your expectations for us as your command staff?"

Ty hesitated. He had difficulty realizing he was a chief, which meant no more racial slurs or jokes. "Loyalty and trust, communication, and leading by example. Both of you have worked in this city for years, and I look forward to your historical experience. My expectation includes not letting me walk into an ambush with department personnel, city hall, or the public. I cannot do this alone. I need your support."

"We will do our very best."

Captain Abel left his office, but Captain Francisco remained to discuss patrol operations.

"Well, Chief, let me say welcome, and I will support you. What are your meeting times, and what day do you want to have as the department staff meeting? FYI, city council meetings are on the second and fourth Tuesdays of every month. When you're ready, I will brief you on the department's structure, personnel, and strategic plans."

"Thank you. I am looking forward to working with you. Let's meet on Thursday morning at about 1000 hours in the conference room."

"Sounds good, sir. I will make sure the lieutenants and day-shift sergeants are present."

Captain Francisco left Ty's office, and Anna came in to discuss procedures.

"How did it go, sir? How are you?"

"Good. The captains discussed many topics," Ty said. "This was a lot on day one. I am looking forward to learning and growing with the department and community.

"I need your assistance in learning my way around the department personnel, city hall, and other agencies. This is a strong learning curve for me. Please be patient with me. I was an army officer, and I tend to be direct sometimes without filters. This is my first experience with an executive secretary. Bear with me."

"No problem, sir. We will do this together."

"Great. I would like to meet with you daily at eight a.m. to discuss upcoming activities and review activities from the day before."

During the conversation, the front desk notified Ty that the IT rep had arrived at the station to set up his computer. Anna instructed the technician on how to set up the computer system. Ty left his office during the setup and visited Captain Francisco.

"Chief, do you have an agenda of the topics to discuss in Thursday's meeting?"

"Not yet. Let me draft an agenda this afternoon and present it to you and Abel."

"Sounds good, sir. Thanks," Captain Francisco said. "Let's take a tour around the city."

"Sure. Let's go."

They walked to the vehicle parking lot, entered an unmarked police car, and toured the city for about forty-five minutes as Francisco described the various neighborhoods.

On his second day, Ty met Anna in his office. He discussed his expectations of her job performance, and she explained how things had been going at the department over the past few years. She was very supportive and helpful to Chief Washington. Anna departed the office, and Ty began setting up his computer files and reviewing PD historical files.

He closed his office door, sat in his high-back leather chair, put his feet on the desk, and leaned back. Ty had finally reached the mountaintop.

His drive home changed as he became a chief. His mind was always racing with thoughts of improving the police department and presenting a more positive face to the community. Ty envisioned how he would like to set up operations; initially, he wouldn't change anything but simply observe and analyze existing operations for about thirty to sixty days.

"Well, how is work going on your first week?" Lorraine asked.

"It was good, and I'm settling in and meeting the employees. I will tell you what is difficult—being called 'sir,' which is very similar to the military. It is very humbling, and yet I feel proud."

"Remember, go slow and listen. Identify those you can trust, who is genuine and sincere, and, most importantly, who is loyal to you!"

"Thank you, honey. Good advice."

Ty watched TV, relaxed, ate dinner, and went to bed early, which was becoming his routine.

The next day came quickly. He arrived early and fired up the computer. His first order of business was to read emails, especially any from the city manager. His strategy was Management by Walking Around (MBWA). Ty enjoyed greeting the employees and telling them what a good job they were doing.

"Morning, Chief. I am Sergeant Fritz, and this is dispatcher Gonzalez."

"Morning. Glad to meet you both. I am eager to support the department as best I can."

Anna arrived for their morning meeting. At ten a.m., they joined Captains Abel and Francisco and Lieutenants Jones and Stanley for the meeting. Ty introduced himself to the lieutenants and shared his background. Each staff member provided introductions to Ty. Remembering never being given expectations as a young police officer, Ty explained his expectations.

Ty's meeting with his police staff was very much like his military staff meetings, and that experience enhanced his ability to exercise positive and reasonable management skills with police staff.

"Communication is the essence of information dissemination," Ty said, addressing the staff. "Please keep me informed when you or your subordinates are contacted by a council member or the city manager. Surprises are not good for anyone. Please support me and don't let me walk into a political ambush. No surprises.

"My goal is to support the mission of our department and all the personnel. I would like to schedule introductions with the other chiefs in the area. Captain Francisco, can you assist me with that?"

"Yes, sir."

"Thank you all for coming to this first staff meeting," Ty said. "We will have one every two weeks until I learn the community and organization."

The meeting concluded, and everyone left the conference room.

Ty returned to his office and reflected on how far he had come in his life. He felt blessed to have become a police chief. He was sad his hero, his mother, hadn't lived long enough to experience his success and perseverance. Ty progressed and began to exercise his plan to make Farmland PD the best police agency in the county.

Next, he wanted to meet community leaders, residents, and business merchants. Over the next several months, Ty made it a weekly objective to visit the local K–12 schools. He met with the principals and several teachers. For many community members, it was the first time they'd ever seen the police chief in a school or inside their business. Ty enjoyed talking to students and emphasizing the importance of education. This was how policing was supposed to be, Ty thought.

Ty began receiving phone calls from a couple of council members. They wanted to know about department goals and questioned him about the conduct of certain police officers. This bother Ty and wasn't protocol. He advised the council members that he couldn't discuss personnel matters with them. For the moment, the phone calls stopped until the mayor began calling and asking the same questions about officers. Ty became uncomfortable and informed the city manager about the phone calls from the council members and mayor.

Bam! Ty had opened Pandora's box. It turned out the council members were questioning police policies and procedures as a mechanism to get rid of the city manager, whom they didn't like. It was politics. The best way to get rid of an appointed official like a police chief or city manager was to allege or falsely accuse, not prove misconduct. The stage was being set for Ty's first lesson in Politics 101; corruption in municipal government comes in many forms, and there is no training manual designed to help police chiefs or city managers. A new dimension was being established, and it wasn't racial harassment but political interference or corruption. Ty and the city manager talked; Ty told him about the phone calls, and the city manager told Ty to be careful. They went to lunch to discuss this pending council issue.

"They are looking for something to make a political issue to get rid of me, and my job is to protect you and the police department from their interference. Listen, Chief, our jobs are political. One wrong word can cost both of us our jobs without any cause or reason. The city council decides on policies and direction for the city, and city managers run the day-to-day operations on behalf of the council. Sometimes there are differences with council direction like in the case of hiring you. I thought another candidate was more qualified than you, as did two other council members. Those are the two calling you. You are a novice. Do not get pulled into the political quicksand.

"Go ahead and talk to them. Just keep me informed every time they call or come to see you. Remember, you work for me, not the mayor or the council."

"Yes, sir, I understand."

They finished lunch. He was concerned about the city manager because of the council members nosing around the police department; he remained cautious. On the bright side, so far so good; no overt or covert signs of racial harassment, slurs, or jokes. Was it because he was now the police chief? A new decade? Had social evolution finally taken hold and racist jokes and behavior disappeared? Ty was learning as a police chief that he needed to know how to maneuver in the treacherous political waters of municipal government. A new twist was added to the policing arsenal: how to avoid political conflict and politicians.

Chief Washington wanted to do a good job in his first police chief position. To do so, he incorporated as much military leadership and college educational training as possible. The theories of personnel behavior became apparent very quickly, and Ty delegated the solution of personnel problems to Captain Abel and patrol problems to Captain Francisco. During the next staff meeting, Ty discussed drafting these plans with both captains.

"Captain Francisco, let's execute our community action plan, invite the key leaders of various businesses here for an open house, and educate them on our operational plans and future of the department."

"Chief, that would be great if we had a plan."

"Really? I would like both you and Captain Abel to develop and write the plan with the input of the lieutenants and sergeants. Let's meet again in two weeks, and by then, an outline should be drafted."

"Okay, sir, but it will be the first time for us," Captain Francisco replied. "We have never been tasked to write a strategic plan or provide input. Please be patient with us."

"No problem. We will work it together."

Ty called a neighboring police chief and discussed his initial assessment and discussions regarding his captains.

"So, Bill, my captains told me they have never been directed to write a strategic plan or establish a task list."

"Well, Ty, one of the reasons you were brought in is because change in operations and procedures was needed," Chief Bill replied. "As you recall, when I sat on your interview panel, your philosophy of planning and community involvement was compelling and the reason you were hired. I knew you were going to have a challenge. Hang in there and bring them along slowly."

"Thanks, Bill. I am realizing my work is cut out for me, and my military leadership experience will be put to the test."

While the captains were working on the plan, Ty reviewed all the historical documents on file. It was puzzling to him that his two senior captains had never written an operations plan or strategic plan. He offered mentoring and assistance to them both.

Home life was good but financially challenging. Lorraine was working, but the cost of living was expanding. Ty's two daughters required financial and moral support. Thus, to supplement his income and professional development, he began teaching criminal justice at a local community college. He enjoyed teaching college and seemed to relate to the students from communities of color. His police and military experience enabled him to provide a wide scope of knowledge to the classes he taught.

The mayor and city council elections were in full swing, and the police department was in the news with police pursuits and the increase in drug crimes. There was a lot going on, including the numerous unresolved Internal Affairs investigations. One of his lieutenants, a subordinate manager, had a number of these investigations in his file records. One of the considerations during the hiring process was whether Ty had enough experience to resolve the allegations of police misconduct and the IAs.

Ty developed a citizen's advisory committee, which consisted of community volunteers who attended a citizens' academy. He briefed the city manager about the committee, and the city manager expressed his pleasure for Ty to take the initiative and establish this committee. He asked Ty to present the establishment of the advisory committee strategy at the next city council meeting.

Ty attended the council meeting and introduced the plan to the council. It was well received by the entire council and supported by public comments during the meeting. The next day, a council member called and asked to meet with Ty for lunch to discuss the merits of the committee. Ty met with him and another council member. And the council member directed Ty not to inform the city manager about the meeting. Ty was very suspicious and uncomfortable; still he met and kept the meeting quiet.

"So, Chief, how are things with the city manager?"

"Fine. I thought we were going to talk about the citizens' committee."

"We will later. Does he interfere in police matters and micromanage you?"

"No, he is very supportive and allows me to manage the department."

For about thirty minutes, these two council members grilled him with questions about the city manager. It was like an informal investigation. Ty held his ground and didn't give in to the council members. The meeting finally ended.

Ty left the restaurant and wondered what the purpose of this meeting was.

Did they want to get rid of the city manager? Ty wondered, *Am I next?*

About two weeks later, the motive was revealed at a regular council meeting. The two council members in open session confronted the city manager about negligent supervision of the police department.

Wow, where is this coming from? What have I walked into? Ty was nervous and realized they were using him to get rid of the city manager.

The following day after the council meeting, Ty went to the city manager and talked to him about the meeting with the council members.

"Chief, I advised you to let me know anytime you talk to council members and to inform me if you do, especially during these rough political times. Last night's council meeting was an example. Did you notice how a couple of them attacked me publicly?"

"Yes, I was shocked and couldn't believe it, and I am telling you now."

"Oh yes, you must realize that when they are finished with me, the same will happen to you," the city manager said. "Heed my words of advice—keep me informed when you get a call or talk to any city council member, including the mayor. I am not going to repeat this to you."

"I understand, sir, just collecting intel. Ty remembered, be politically astute but not politically active, but I did believe their interest was genuine."

"Ty, politicians are demons, and you are not familiar with this type of political warfare."

The next few weeks were challenging because of the inherited IAs Ty had to resolve. The investigations centered on police misconduct and were being investigated by the lieutenant. The investigations were completed and submitted to the administrative sergeant who submitted to Ty for punishment decision.

"Sergeant, set up appointments for the officers so I can provide them with the deposition," Ty told one of his sergeants. "So much time has passed, and I do not want them to worry any longer than necessary."

"Sounds good, Chief. Will do."

No matter how many times he was called "Chief," it sounded strange and awkward. Ty didn't realize he had been traumatized by the years of racial harassment but kept his emotions under control when dealing with his officers.

The next two weeks were challenging but rewarding. Ty completed the IAs and, in conjunction with the captains, drafted the department strategic plan. He brought the captains into his office to discuss his direction in accordance with the plan.

"Gentlemen, I have reviewed the drafts you completed, and we need to plan our timelines. Sections one and two deal with personnel issues, including evaluations and chain of command. I want to make sure the evaluations have measurable and tangible benchmarks and accomplishments."

"Chief, in the past we only wrote a few pages on evaluations, and there was no established procedure."

"We are going to change that," Ty affirmed. "We owe to the personnel objective and measurable standards upon which to provide them with career guidance. Chapters three through six discuss our community policing and logistical directions. The six-chapter strategic plan is a work in progress. We will continue to discuss them. Have a great rest of your day."

Both captains left his office.

Wow, the army really was a great learning environment, Ty thought. *No one ever discussed strategic planning at my previous departments.*

Ty felt good. He was able to provide leadership and essential knowledge to his officers at Farmland PD, despite the years of past humiliation and discrimination against him.

Ty was an "at will" employee of the city. This meant he could be fired without cause. There was no severance packet to provide him with a few months of salary and benefits. If he upset the council or the city manager, termination didn't have to be fair and impartial. He had no due-process protection. The city council meetings were held every two weeks. Basically, Ty knew he was up for termination or reappointment at every council meeting, which wasn't a good feeling.

During a closed session at one of the council meetings, the mayor and the council members made a surprising decision. The five council members exited the meeting and announced they had voted to terminate Ty's contract as police chief with a 3–2 vote. The two council members who had been talking to Ty were the two dissenting or opposing votes. The mayor and two other council members made up the majority vote. This was very shocking to everyone, including Ty. There had been no warning signs or indicators this was going to happen as an "at will" employee to Ty.

He later learned the council had justified the firing because of an unsanctioned meeting with other council members. It was alleged that Ty had discussed city matters outside regulatory council meetings. He didn't violate any law or procedure in the city regulations; he only pissed off the council majority.

Ty also learned the city manager had stabbed him in the back by going to the council majority and telling them about the meeting as well; so much for confidentiality and loyalty. The move by the city manager was to divert the council attention away from firing him (Municipal Politics 101A). The city manager had orchestrated Ty's demise, and the entire time Ty had been trying to protect him. Many community members expressed disbelief and concern in response to the council's action, but they had no effect on the vote to terminate Ty.

On his last day, police department personnel were silent, only saying, "Good luck, Chief." Ty thought he was a good chief and would have received more support from the personnel. Well, later he discovered the treachery from within, where some of his command staffers (captain, lieutenants) had gone to the city manager and expressed their displeasure with Ty's management style. Yes, another backstabbing, and the pattern was clear to him; he wasn't called racial names, and there weren't racial jokes made, but the outcome the same. He had known that when he accepted this golden opportunity (and none of the command staff were Black), it would be a struggle. Ty hadn't really thought about it until the termination notice was made; then it all made sense. Some of the department officers were loyal to

Ty, which was revealed to him some weeks later when he met some of the officers at a local coffee shop.

"Sir," said Officer Noble, "you were approachable, fair, and genuine. Some of the command staff didn't like that and started talking trash on you to the city manager. It was common knowledge you were being betrayed."

"So why didn't one of you tell me?"

"Sir, it would have been career suicide, because chiefs come and go. Those captains, lieutenants, and sergeants remain."

"Thank you. Take care of yourselves and always do the right thing for the right reason!" Ty finished his coffee and left the coffee shop, never to return.

Ty talked with a fellow Black chief and expressed his dismay at what had happened. Ty's termination was in the local newspaper, adding insult to injury. "Ty, I heard council was looking for a way to get rid of you because you were too progressive and very community minded. That meant the status quo police officers couldn't intimidate the community because you were the social justice police chief.

"We heard about various comments regarding that 'Black chief,' only they didn't say 'Black.' One of your sergeants was overheard complaining to certain officers that having a Black man in charge was degrading and ruined the department's reputation. One of the lieutenants was heard making a comment about how demeaning it was to have a descendant of slaves running our beloved police department.

"On many occasions, they both made racial jokes and slurs about the 'Black sambo' running a police agency," he said. I was fearful of losing my job and didn't even think about telling you for fear of retaliation as well."

Ty later had a couple of the officers come to him and corroborated these comments by the sergeant and lieutenant.

As a chief of police, the lesson Ty learned was that racism still exists, and political lynching takes place in twentieth-century policing.

CHAPTER 11

Faith Forged under Fire
Metro Police Department

On the road again! Ty thought, stunned, dismayed, and quite depressed about Farmland PD. He looked at those experiences in the rearview mirror. *Law enforcement is a much more difficult profession than he thought.* He was determined not to make the same mistakes at his next chief position at a new agency. To start with, he met and talked at length with several of the local police chiefs.

All discussed the possibility of the same political circus in their respective cities and the nuclear option, the "vote of no confidence" by the police union.

One chief told Ty, "You are elected chief and exist only from council meeting to council meeting, because things can literally change overnight." This was true sarcasm since 90 percent of police chiefs were appointed and not elected. The statement reflected the belief that a police chief would be here today before the council meeting and could be gone the next day after the council meeting. It wasn't a fair system.

Ty wouldn't quit. He enrolled in a master's program in management at a local university. One of the classes discussed the fact that the average tenure of a police chief in the United States was about 2.7 to 3.2 years. Clearly there were those chiefs who were blessed with the right city manager, city council, and positive police union. Although it was the era of community-oriented policing (COP), the community's input on the performance of a police chief didn't appear to matter.

Another class discussed management in the political arena, which was where most police chiefs lived. There was a theory called the "three-legged stool" of a police chief: one leg was the city council, one leg was the city manager, and one leg was the police union. Losing one leg could cause a police chief to fall.

Once again, he called on the U.S. Army and signed up for a two-year tour. The army was a sanctuary, a true professional environment focused on performance and skill rather than on race. In two years, Ty finished his law degree and was ready to take on racism and politics. He returned to seeking the role of police chief and realized the intensive scrutiny he would undergo in his return bid, but others had survived the political scrutiny of a background investigation.

The truth of the matter was that the racial harassment and hostile environment he had experienced early in his career wasn't a defense in a background investigation. He would be an incompetent, ineffective, poor, and thin-skinned manager—someone with a chip on his shoulder—and race was always the excuse for his behavior.

His personnel files wouldn't reflect the racial hostility he experienced as a young cop or the institutional or hidden racism he saw as chief. "No surrender, no retreat!" was Ty's rallying cry.

After several months of applying and interviewing, Metro Police Department, a moderate-sized police department, hired him. He arrived at Metro City Hall and met his new boss, the city manager.

"Greetings and welcome, Chief Washington. My name is Tom, and I want to welcome you to the city of Metro. I know we have talked on the phone, but I want to formally extend an invitation to hire you. Please sign this form. Let's have a frank conversation. This place is a hot mess of political turmoil. The last chief only lasted six months, and the one before him eight months."

"Yes, sir, I have read the news articles and watched various TV news channels that covered the story."

"I know you had political turmoil in your last chief position, but you have integrity and an ethical backbone, which we need here. You were dragged through the mud. In many cases that is normal for police chiefs in toxic governmental communities. Welcome to another one. Quite frankly, we didn't think anyone would risk their career to come here."

"Sir, I have experienced some major sociopolitical and racial turmoil in my law enforcement career. I do not give up, and I fight on."

Hmm, thought Ty. *This city manager appears to sympathize with me, but I have crossed this road before.*

"Chief, I reviewed your background investigation summary, and hopefully you learned not to trust council members. Your best friend really is me, the city manager—or it should be. I recommended to the entire council to hire you over the other final applicants."

"Thank you, sir."

"Just remember, always communicate with me on any contact you have with any council members. We will survive the politics together."

"Sir, I like your style."

"Chief, I am sending you to a two-week executive management course, where they will talk about city government and how to deal with toxic political environments. I believe the course starts next month. I will keep you posted."

"Thank you, sir. I appreciate your support, and I need you to support me as well."

Ty left the city manager's office and walked across the city hall courtyard to the police department. Both captains met him.

"Morning, Chief. I am Captain Provost, field operations manager."

"I am Captain Markus, the administrative manager."

"Nice to meet you both," Ty said as they escorted him to his office.

"Chief, you come highly recommended. Captain Markus and I are looking forward to your guidance and direction. We have an interesting group of officers here—some good cops, some not so good."

"Yes," Markus, added. "We have quite a few Internal Affairs investigations. You know cops sometimes get into trouble while arresting crooks but sometimes through misconduct off duty."

"I understand. It is interesting that our initial conversations are about IA investigations rather than community policing, strategic planning, and future development of personnel."

"Sir, you know it is always the ten percent who use ninety percent of your time."

"Chief, we understand you are going to executive management training for law enforcement executive officials. We have both attended the course. We will update some department documents for you to review when you return from the course."

"Sounds good. How about a quick spin around the department?"

"No problem, sir."

They walked through the first and second floors of the police building and met with several employees and returned to Ty's office.

"Thank you both for the tour of the department," Ty said. "I'm looking forward to working with you both. Tomorrow I would like to drive around the city and meet some merchants and visit some of the schools."

"Fine, sir, but I advise you to take it slow," said Captain Provost.

"You're right. Thank you. I'm heading home soon and will see you both in tomorrow."

"Good night, sir."

Ty drove home and explained his first day to his wife.

"Can't wait until tomorrow!" Ty told her. "I am exhausted. It looks like the same political nightmare, but the city manager appears to care and wants me to be successful."

"I hear you. Let's see."

He kissed his wife, and they went to bed.

He arrived to work early and met his executive secretary, Diane. They talked about administrative procedures and his office files.

"Well, Chief, welcome," she said. "There is a lot going on, and I will help you as much as possible."

"Thank you, Diane. I appreciate that. I just want to be a good leader and role model for all police employees."

"*Pues*, Chief, I hear you speak Spanish."

"*Si, por su puesto*. Yes, of course. I enjoy the culture and language and learned to speak Spanish as a young child."

After Ty met with his executive secretary, Captain Provost escorted him around the city. They stopped to meet a few business owners, many of whom spoke only Spanish. Ty was able to speak with the business owners and learned they had never met the chief of police after maintaining their business in the city for more than fifteen years. After a couple of hours and two coffee stops, they returned to the station.

"Thank you for the tour of the city, Captain. I would like to spend the rest of the week meeting the officers and department staff. I will meet a few this week and when I return from the executive course in two weeks."

Ty traveled to the executive management course in Sacramento, California. The course was structured similarly to a college graduate course. The attendees were assigned to write a course term paper. It was time for Ty to apply the sixteen years of police work, five years of teaching, and sixteen years of experience as an army officer to the development and writing of this strategy. Ty's term paper was titled "Policing and Racial Tensions."

Ty looked at several events with substantial racial overtones, notwithstanding his own personal experiences: the shootings of Eula Love in 1979 and Latasha Harlins by a Korean store owner in March 1991 and the Rodney King beating in 1991, several other events, and the analysis of Jim Crow laws, which formalized racial discrimination in the United States. Ty believed in the emerging community-oriented policing (COP) philosophy. This philosophy was becoming a standard in policing, but many officers didn't like COP because they believed they were giving in to the complaints of minority communities—in other words, communities of color. Some primarily White officers believed COP was capitulation and displayed weakness.

Ty's management course paper discussed the importance of COP, and he listened to the community's concerns of their respective police department. His paper emphasized consensus leadership, where police executive leaders should listen to and take care of the needs of subordinate officers. He referenced his early experiences in policing when he was the victim of racial slurs, jokes, and harassment by fellow police officers and supervisors.

He met with a classmate to discuss the turning in of this paper. "So, John, my paper is on racial discrimination in policing, not against the community but rather internally. I had supervisors using the n-word and telling degrading racial jokes."

"Terrible behavior by our colleagues in policing," John said. "The thought that you were treated so degradingly when some of the same officers arrested and used excessive force against people of color is unconscionable. What is the purpose of your paper?"

"I want to show how American history has promoted this distrust against police and how pervasively it is when a fellow police officer is treated in a manner that is so defamatory. The lessons learned may keep another Black, Hispanic, or female officer from experiencing the hostility I felt for years. Moreover, I'm hoping this changes this behavior to truly reflect freedom and justice for all."

Ty turned in his course paper and received praise from the instructor for having the guts to write about such a controversial and sensitive topic.

Ty returned to Metro PD and scheduled a staff meeting with his captains and lieutenants. Ty was still having problems in his mind transitioning from being the young Black cop, who was a regular target of racial injustice by his fellow police officers, to a Black chief of police with duties and responsibilities for a community. Ty was extremely honored and used every ounce of his military officer training to help with the transition to success.

He was eager to share the knowledge of the training and his expectations for the future of the police department. The meeting started at one p.m., and he presented his expectations, organizational direction, and mission objectives.

"It is not my intent to become involved in the present political turmoil of the city but rather to support the police department in performing our sworn duties."

"Chief, I have to be honest," one lieutenant said. "This is a good department with good personnel, but we have had some political conflicts and uncertainty over the last two years. I won't go into it too deeply right now, but we hope you will support the police department and not city hall."

"I appreciate your candor, and we will work together for the good of the community and the personnel on this police department. I am a strong advocate of community-oriented policing and believe in statistical analysis for crime mapping. It is my intent to review and evaluate the department before any major changes or modifications take place."

"We appreciate that, sir."

"I do expect my command staff, all of you here, to keep me informed. Remember to provide me with written memorandums of issues requiring my attention."

"No problem, sir. We will work together."

After two hours, the meeting concluded.

As they walked down the hallway, Captain Provost said, "You know, Chief, I didn't mean to come off so direct, but Markus and I have been dealing with city hall improprieties for several years, and we want to make sure you are not part of their plan to dominate the police department."

"Captain, I've had my battles with city government and internal police personnel due to politics and improprieties in city hall. I get it."

Williams nodded, inferring he understood.

His executive secretary and they talked about overall police operations.

"Sir, I'm sure by now you have heard about the political scandals that have plagued the city and police department for the past few years."

"Yes, I have. And my goals are to manage and lead the police department the best I can to ensure quality delivery of police services."

"Sounds good, sir, but just be aware. The city manager and city council may try to manipulate you, and the police union will be a constant thorn in your side."

"Thank you. I appreciate the heads-up, and I'll keep it in mind. Would you bring me last year's budget and department annual reports?"

"Yes, sir. Give me a few minutes."

"No problem. I have plenty to do."

Ty hit the ground running, focusing on administrative systems, and didn't want to take the usual ninety days to access and evaluate police operations before affecting change. The city manager contacted him within a few days for coffee at Starbucks. The city manager discussed the hornet's nest Ty had accepted by becoming chief.

"Unethical conduct of some of your staff has been reported to me and the council members," the city manager began. "There is a substantial political divide between the council, police union, and some community members. You were hired by the council to fix the PD."

"I appreciate the confidence, but I will do what is ethical and lawful to promote a positive police department image. I will do a top-to-bottom analysis of operations to ensure police policies are in accordance with the city's general plan. I will also start drafting a five-year strategic plan with the input of the police employees, community, and city government."

"I like what you are saying, Chief. Just remember to watch your back. Many of the police department personnel didn't support your hiring, and they'll jump at any opportunity to prove you wrong."

"Thank you, sir. I appreciate the insight."

"Chief, we will work through these challenging times together."

"Sir, I am not generally a police union loyalist," Ty said. "I believe the purpose and mission of the police unions have really changed from protecting the due process rights of police officers to challenging all management decisions, both operational and administrative."

"I hear you, Chief. Watch out for the vipers. They are there! Let's have coffee regularly to share progress on resolving the concerns."

What the hell have I walked into? Ty thought as he went home. I have already dealt with a tumultuous police department. I'm not going to deal with another one! I guess I have been identified as a change agent, and this is going to take all of my abilities.

Now it had begun. The mayor invited Ty to lunch, and he notified the city manager right away. Ty and the mayor sat down at the local Denny's.

"So how are things?" the mayor asked.

"It is challenging," Ty responded. "A lot of issues to deal with, but I am ready to handle them."

"Listen, Chief Washington, I may need some support from you in my next election. You need to make sure all your officers are doing their jobs, especially your command staff captains and lieutenants. I can't go into details, but we, the council majority, brought you in to clean up the police department."

Ty listened. Though he wasn't exactly sure what the mayor was talking about, he tried changing the subject.

"Mr. Mayor, we are looking at purchasing new police cars and maybe hiring two or three more officers."

"Listen, Chief, watch what you say to council members Bill and Ted because they didn't want to hire you. They talk weekly to your police union about your movements and changes. I think they are keeping a book on your actions so they can get rid of you when the time is right."

Not again!

"That doesn't make sense to me. That is the opposite message I am seeing in the department," Ty said, but he never mentioned his discussions with the city manager. "Thanks, Mayor, I appreciate the heads-up."

"Here is my cell phone number, Chief. Call me anytime. I want you to be successful. Call me whenever you want, and let's stay in touch."

"Thank you, sir."

Ty was totally confused. *Why is the mayor of the city talking to me about such sensitive information?*

As a new police chief, he wasn't sure how to handle the situation, so he just kept it quiet. Ty thought he had learned and would be ready after the experiences at Farm PD. He now had two chief jobs with political turmoil and tumultuous city governments in his résumé. He was responsible for everything, including the conduct of every employee—from the nonsworn dispatchers to the police officers and his subordinate leaders.

He called an entire police department staff meeting to discuss goals and objectives. "Captain Provost, what is the training plan for the next year for our officers?"

"Well, Chief, as you know, POST, or peace officer standards training, outlines the requirements, and I am trying to schedule officers for training. It's difficult. Officers are either going on vacation, calling in sick, or working massive overtime. To answer your question, we have no training plan."

"Okay, I would like you to draft a plan, and we will review it in a few weeks."

"Sounds good, sir. Will do."

The meeting concluded, and Ty returned to his office and began reviewing those files in his office from the previous chief. He wondered how loyal some of his officers were to the police department. Some of the officers were more interested in personal concerns and not those of the community. Ty moved forward to establish a positive organizational culture where working together as a team was the primary objective.

Doing community projects, visiting the schools, and working with the local merchants to establish community neighborhood watch groups were among Ty's key projects. The two captains and lieutenants performed various administrative day-to-day tasks. During the department staff meeting, Ty assigned various projects and reports to determine the readiness of the police department. Some of the projects were very labor intensive and required months to research and complete.

Ty was a true community chief. He visited and met with many groups, from the local city schools to the chamber of commerce. He loved to visit schools and talk with schoolkids. He went to a fifth-grade class and talked to the students about education.

"Be sure to study and take schoolwork serious," Ty began. "Do not be afraid to read a book at home instead of watching TV. Remember to respect everyone—teachers, friends, and, of course, your parents."

Even though Ty had finished one year at Metro PD, he knew he was on borrowed time. It was only a matter of time before the political turmoil in the city reached him. He was satisfied with the direction of the police department. As the political stress mounted, Ty felt the stress between city hall and the police department, and he began taking some of it home. The first casualty for Ty was his marriage to Lorraine; slowly they drifted apart. He worked longer, and she worked longer hours at her job. Although he really wanted to be a good husband, the arguments increased at home as pressure mounted at work.

Finally, they divorced. Ty wasn't happy. Two divorces in ten years weren't a good average. Despite his success in the community, the drums of internal discontent began. The police union became bolder and directly approached city council members and the city manager, complaining that they didn't like the direction of the police department and that the chief wasn't a team player.

"The chief is always visiting the homes, schools, and businesses in the community instead of staying in the office and helping us officers," a rep from the police union complained.

Ty needed to discuss his concerns and could do so only with other chiefs, so he reached out to Chief Jack from another local agency.

"Hey, Jack, my police union is becoming very vocal by going behind my back to complain about me to council members."

"That is bullshit. They should not be allowed to speak with the council under the guise of union business. There is protocol, and the union should adhere to it as well," Chief

Jack responded. "Ty, I guess you now know who is loyal and who is not. Continue to work on organizational issues and let the union do their thing."

"You're right, but it is a distraction. I will have to work through this challenge."

"Well, Ty, your problem is no different from that of most chiefs. I just hope your city manager and council believe in you and will back you one hundred percent. Get to the city manager and let him know what is going on. He can be your greatest advocate."

"That's true," Ty confirmed. "So far, he is on board. We've discussed the situation, and he isn't concerned at this time."

"Not concerned? Well, keep your eye on the ball and stay informed."

"Thanks, Jack. Will do."

Later in the week, Ty called and met with two other chiefs.

Chief Joe posed an interesting question. "Do you think some of the officers are creating these complaints because you are the only Black police chief in the history of this city and have only a few Black officers who are too intimidated to say a word?"

"I don't think so," Ty replied. "But you never know."

"Be mindful, Ty. Unions have a habit of targeting certain chiefs and voting no confidence, which is the nuclear option, as a union political ploy to get rid of them. The worst part is, generally there is no basis for the no-confidence vote (nuclear option). They solicit city council support by giving the letter to council through backdoor channels instead of through the formal chain-of-command method. Department policies require the officers to go through the police department before procedurally going to the city manager or council. They did not!"

The officers were complaining that Ty was holding them to strict compliance with department policy and didn't like all the community-oriented policing initiatives since it appeared to favor citizens, not police officers. The city manager discussed the complaints with Ty, and he realized the conflict. The union members expressed their desire for higher pay and more benefits, yet they were telling selected council members and the city manager they didn't appreciate Ty's direct management style. Ty's leadership style was based on mission accomplishment through the best delivery of police services to the community. Negotiations proved positive, and Ty helped broker the settlement with the union.

Some of the police officers had a reputation for being aggressive and hostile to citizens. There were several complaints filed against some of the officers, and many citizens felt harassed by the large number of citations issued. Racial profiling became a very important issue for law enforcement. Some of the complaints alleged that officers stopped Hispanic and Black citizens at a higher rate than Whites. Ty assigned the IA sergeant to investigate the racial profiling allegations, and, if substantiated, the officer would be held accountable.

Chief Ty believed in his officers, and the few bad apples shouldn't cause the entire department to be judged unfairly. Therefore, accountability of officer conduct was key to a positive police image. There were times when Chief Ty disciplined some of the officers, which invoked representation by the union. Based on the harassment and mistreatment he'd experienced as a young police officer, Ty tended to be more lenient on disciplining but remained fair.

Ty reflected on his earlier days in policing when he was ridiculed, experienced racial harassment, and worked in a hostile environment. There had been no support for him or due process. Ty wouldn't repeat this behavior to his officers; he believed that fairness in accordance with the law would prevail.

The filing of citizen complaints was an important management and agency tool. The law protected citizens and police officers from unfair or fictitious complaints. In an effort to manage the citizen complaints and foster a community-oriented policing atmosphere, Ty required that Captains Provost and Markus closely monitor how the investigated officer performed patrol functions due to the high volume of alleged police misconduct. This included reviewing all "use of force" complaints to ensure fairness to all parties.

Ty was often direct; for example, certain veteran officers arrived late to work or failed to turn in reports on time. He established a system where the sergeants maintained a record to ensure accountability and ensure reports and other personal habits met department standards. Many officers didn't favor this system. He didn't feel he was mistreating or harassing the officers; he was only holding them accountable for their conduct and performance. Some of the officers, who believed he was abusing his power as chief, emphatically disagreed.

His discussions with the city manager escalated. The complaints regarding use of force and verbal abuse didn't slow down.

"Ty, I am receiving more and more complaints against your officers. I need you to be more assertive."

"Fine, sir. Let's do an audit and review the complaints. I think findings will establish we are accomplishing our organizational mission. Sir, the council members are not supposed to talk to the officers about complaints within the police department," Ty emphasized. "Protocol requires they bring them to me via the city manager. Police chiefs have the authority to manage their departments without intervention by the city manager or council. Therefore, a police chief is appointed and not elected like sheriffs."

Ty went to lunch with a chief from a nearby city, who had become a good friend.

"So, Chief Beto, do you have a love-hate relationship with your police union?" Ty asked.

"Of course! Many chiefs do. We have evolved so much in police work that some police unions want political control of the department to neutralize the chief's authority. This is dangerous because if the union can be controlled by a governing body, police management cannot effectively lead the organization.

"Imagine a situation where elected officials can dictate how an independent agency of trained law enforcement officers can be manipulated by untrained, uneducated, or inexperienced governing bodies like city council. There would be no need for a police chief."

"I agree." Ty nodded. "They act as if they hired a puppet and I keep trying to cut the string."

"It can get even uglier," Chief Beto said. "If there are some unethical officers in a department who are self-serving, they will attempt—and in some cases be successful—at manipulating a new rookie city official. Then that officer or group of officers can pull off a coup to betray and usurp the authority of the chief. It's a nasty business."

"But Beto, what if you know that ethically, legally, and morally you are doing the right thing for the community? Why worry? I'm trying hard not to let the union or individual members exercise management in situations they are not educated or trained to understand. Isn't that why a city council and city manager appoint a police chief in the first place?"

"Yes, Ty, you are correct. Except it doesn't matter. Think back to the chiefs' training conference when we discussed the intermeddling of council members into police affairs. Therefore, the law is specific on police chiefs exercising exclusive control over the police department. But if council members are persuaded for whatever reason to turn against you, they will!"

"Yeah, I guess that right and wrong have nothing to do with this. It's a simple matter of subjective feelings."

"It's sad to say, Ty, but some elected officials just worry about getting elected. Meanwhile, police unions provide strong political allies at election time, and some even contribute to the campaigns of officials."

"I have seen that in my career," commented Ty. "I strongly believe in fairness and due process, but this is different."

"Ty, the composition of your agency is different from mine," Chief Beto added. "The members of my police union are educated and experienced police officers, who care about the community and the department. On the other hand, you hired some officers I wouldn't have hired, and now you've inherited the baggage that comes with that risk. They are malcontents stirring the pot! Remember, it's the caliber of the persons you hire that determines the level of experience, competency, skills, and ethical loyalty of that department."

"Thanks, Beto. I appreciate your time."

"Hang in there, Ty. You can pull through this ordeal if rational thought is used by your council and city manager."

"Yeah, don't bet on that. I do not trust the council."

To Ty, his talk with Chief Beto had been a powerful discussion. Beto's words rang true, but the situation didn't improve. Ty spoke with another police chief friend, Charleston. They often shared issues and concerns about being a police chief. Discipline was a task that requires legal acumen, objective thought, and some elbow grease. It was well known that police chiefs couldn't share their plight with anyone, except other police chiefs.

"I understand, and there are many examples," replied Chief Charleston. "We must walk the line and make sure we protect the rights of the officers, even though they will cut our throats. Loyalty in police work is not like it was when we were young cops. You didn't whine and complain because you didn't like the boss—you sucked it up and did your job."

"I agree with you," Ty responded. "But it was a bit different for me coming up as a young officer. I tried very hard to be a good cop, but I had to deal with racial disparity and harassment."

"I hear you, Ty. The '70s and '80s weren't good times for Black officers," Chief Charleston affirmed. "Being a White guy, I cannot possibly understand how you feel."

"Yeah, things are so much better now, and hopefully we never revisit that era in policing. Talk to you later, Charleston."

Through it all, Ty maintained his faith in Jesus Christ. God was always with him; even during the times when he felt alone, he was never alone. Ty's love of education drove him to focus on higher education. His struggle with racial discrimination and political corruption had provided him with an excellent resource base to help others. Ty dedicated his life to mentoring and coaching young people as much as possible, no matter where the future led him.

Ty lived at Metro PD, and despite the constant political pressure, he developed some innovative regional law enforcement strategies. In concert with some area city police chiefs—including Charleston, Billy, and his FBI friends Joe and Galveston—he put together a regional task force. The task force concept of operations was to incorporate all levels of law enforcement into one team, which would conduct regional drug- and gang-related operations. It consisted of federal, state, national, and municipal law enforcement agencies.

The FBI, DEA, ATF, and ICE comprised these federal agencies. The federal representatives were coordinated through Ty's FBI friend. Joe and Ty had the same operational beliefs about joint regional police actions directed at disrupting criminal enterprises, and both believed in crime reduction and prevention. The state troopers, county sheriff, and every municipal police agency comprised this high-speed task force.

Next on Ty's professional development list was law school. He enrolled at a local law school and spent many nights writing and studying law. To be free of criticism, he didn't tell anyone he was attending law school. He balanced being a police chief and the management of Metro PD and his personal development in law school. If this wasn't enough, Ty attended an executive leadership course in Quantico, Virginia, at the FBI headquarters. During his absence from the police department, Captain Provost was appointed acting chief.

He was able to do his homework for law school via the internet. Technology was great, and Ty maintained his grades while completing the course. This first year in law school was complex and filled to the brim with criminal law, torts, and real property. Ty spent hours writing of case briefs, reading the hornbooks (exact rules of law), and writing lecture notes. When class finished each day, Ty and the other chiefs went out to dinner and discussed many issues.

"Ty, you were talking the other day about some sort of test all police chiefs should be aware of," Chief John said.

"Yes, I call it the four- or three-pronged test or 'four legs of a stool' test. One leg is the city manager, the second leg is the mayor and city council members, and the third leg is the police union—and in some cities, the second-chance syndrome (SCS). The distinction between a three- or four-legged stool depends on the agency. Some agencies are not second-chance agencies; in effect, they don't hire cops who have been fired by other agencies (a.k.a. the problem officers of another agency).

"The test goes like this: if one of the three or four legs is removed, the stool will probably fall. In the case of a three-legged stool, that's game over. It will fall. With a four-legged stool, it may fall. Remember, the mayor and council consist of one leg, the city manager consists of another leg, and the police union consists of a third leg."

"Ty," replied Chief Richard, "I agree with your theory. My city is a four-pronged city because we do not hire second-chance officers."

"My stool has three legs because we rarely hire an officer who has problems at other agencies," Chief Greg replied. "Remember, in smaller police agencies, SCS are more common because they generally pay less and need officers."

"Yes, I hear you," Ty said.

Ty finished his dinner with his police chief friends and returned home. After his dinner, he decided to enroll in a police executive training course. After completing the training course, on the plane he wrote notes regarding the "police chief sitting stool" test and SCS. In Ty's case, he had inherited SCS officers, but he had also hired a few. Ty knew America was about opportunities and chances, but sometimes this human desire to help can backfire, especially in police work. There were various schools of thought about second-chance officers. Some appreciated the chance and excelled; others continued the type of behavior that had led to their demise at the first agency.

The second-chance syndrome (SCS) is interesting and can probably be considered a variable, depending on the agency and the individual. This concept is generally connected to another sub concept of "injustice collectors" (IC). These are organizational individuals who collect all negative information and never forget or forgive. They are sometimes referred to as "organizational terrorists."

As he landed at LAX on a Sunday afternoon, he looked out the plane's window, saw the famous LAX structure, and thought, *Okay, I am back home. Will I make a difference in policing?*

He returned to work on Monday morning, met with Captains Provost and Markus, and discussed the SCS and "three-legged stool" concept.

"Chief, I have heard these concepts before, and I believe they are real," Captain Provost said.

"Yes, I agree, Chief," Captain Markus said.

"Good discussion, but let's review the IAs and brief on what has occurred during my absence," Ty said.

"Chief, we have concluded six of the eight IAs and need you to have the disciplinary hearing with these officers."

"Fine. Let's schedule the hearings over the next few weeks and complete the investigations."

Ty completed the disciplinary hearings, issued the punishment, and returned to his true love of the job—community-oriented policing.

He continued to visit local business leaders, school officials, and chamber of commerce members. Ty noticed that some of the officers continued to believe the community members should serve them and that community policing was too much a public relations strategy and not real policing. Chief Washington was determined to change that mindset and persuade the officers to think about the community first.

Ty sat on the beach and analyzed where he was in life and how far he had traveled. After a few hours at the beach, he met his brothers and shared these thoughts with them.

"The many years of training, education, and experience in law enforcement are a true career multiplier. The US Army, policing, and higher education have been the life choices for me. Since I was a police chief, the issues were more political than racial. The corruption in municipal government is shocking because it's not always fraud and embezzlement, but it can be nepotism-like decisions, which have the appearance of impropriety.

"My faith in the Lord Jesus strengthened me throughout the trials and tribulations of life, especially during the difficult times in police work. Taking things to God in prayer provided relief and a private sanctuary. Whatever your belief, having one is really the essence of faithful living and personal peace.

"Being promoted to an executive level in police work was never a thought or goal of mine, but it was truly an honor. Life experiences provide tools to success. This includes having positive mentors and life coaches along the way. I became a police chief against all odds, and when you look at the numbers of African American police chiefs in the larger states, such as Texas, California, and New York, you understand the dilemma."

CHAPTER 12

Fighting the Good Fight
Metro Police Department

Chief Ty really enjoyed talking to students in schools. He walked into the lobby of George Washington Middle School and met the principal and vice principal. Grace was the vice principal, and Sally was the principal. He met both in the front office.

"Morning, Chief. It is good to have you come by the school. It is so nice to see a police chief who practices community-oriented policing," Grace said.

"Thank you," replied Ty. "I would like to increase a positive police presence on campus and let the students see the police as their friends and mentors."

"That sounds great. One of your officers comes by the school weekly, and we discuss various student issues and educational opportunities. As you know, we do have various juvenile concerns like gangs, drugs, and bullying. Would you like to visit a few classrooms and talk to some students?"

"Yes, it is important for the students to see the police chief in their classroom and understand they are just as important as anyone in the city. I want to express to them the importance of making the right choices and have hope that no matter how poor they may be, success is always a possibility."

"Sounds good, Chief. We will put together a schedule and contact your secretary."

"Are there any specific audiovisuals or other support equipment needed?" Grace asked.

"No, thank you," Ty said. "This is just a chance for me to meet with the students so they can get an up-close-and-personal audience with the chief."

"I think this is great," Sally commented. "Previous chiefs have never visited the schools."

"I am happy and honored to share with our greatest natural resource, our children."

"Would you like to drop in on a class now, just to say hi?"

"Sure, that works for me."

"Fine. I know just the class."

They walked to a classroom of forty-plus students, and when Ty entered in full police uniform, the students stopped talking immediately.

"What happened?" asked one student.

The principal introduced Chief Tyrone Washington and explained his intention to provide support to students.

"Good morning, class. I want to let you know that as your police chief, I represent everyone who lives and works in the city. In the next few months, I plan to visit the schools on a regular basis to talk to you about staying out of gangs, drugs, and bullying."

"Class, the chief believes in supporting education and likes to coach football," the principal stated.

"Yes." Ty nodded. "It is important for all of you to focus on your education, and one tool is sports. I played football in high school, and it led to a good career in policing and the military. I'll share more on my next visit."

Sally thanked the chief, and they left the classroom; and once outside, she expressed her gratitude for the visit.

"Thank you, Chief. I have been principal for six years, and we have never met or seen the police chief. The staff appreciates your efforts. Again, thank you."

"It was a pleasure."

Ty returned to his office and discussed the school visit with Captain Provost. "Captain Provost, we need to increase our presence at the schools in a positive way by assigning police officers to the school campuses as school resource officers (SROs) with the mission of prevention, intervention, and mentoring students."

"Fine, Chief, we can do that," Captain Provost responded. "But understand that we do not have the funding for those positions. Also remember the political conflicts with the police union, who has the ear of two council members. Chief, the police union doesn't like your community-policing approach. They prefer the 'kick ass and take names' police strategy."

"Fine, but as long as I am chief, the community residents and our police mission come first."

"Yes, sir, we will continue to make things better for our community."

Captain Provost left Ty's office, and he continued reading the Internal Affairs investigations and updating

Ty. He was gearing up for another round of politics, and the first round fired at Ty was once again from the city manager. He started questioning Ty constantly about the status of internal investigations, disciplines, strategic plans, and other internal police operations.

"Chief, tell me about your plans for increasing the staffing of your department," the city manager began.

"I need funding to increase staffing and plans for community events like the festivals and school resource officers."

Ty was confused by the sudden change in the city manager's demeanor. Ty felt like he was turning on him. The questions were very specific and detailed, indicating he was receiving info from within the department. Ty knew someone had leaked to the city manager but didn't know whom to trust. Yes, there was a rat in his kitchen. Ty knew certain union members talked with the city manager, but the manager always told Ty. This suddenly stopped, and Ty knew they were still talking to him.

Ty met with his captains to discuss how to deal with the forecast of thunder and other "politically inclement weather" looming on the horizon.

"Captain Provost, how do we deal with the union going behind our back to the city manager and council?"

"Chief, Captain Markus and I have discussed this issue, and we like your approach of just being honest and direct with the issues. The officers don't like all this community stuff you've been implementing, and they're itching to kick ass and take names. Your community outreach approach makes some officers think you are more sensitive to the community needs than theirs."

"Captain, let me again clarify my philosophy. My officers and every employee of this police department are important. I will always support them. But the officers need to understand the concept of 'Mission First, People Always.' Our mission is to provide the effective delivery of police services to the community, whether it is a law enforcement operation involving criminal arrests or speaking to schoolchildren about gangs and drugs."

"Chief, I understand," Captain Provost said. "I only offer some insight to help you strategize. The officers are actually talking to me and expressing their concerns."

"I appreciate the heads-up, but we need to ensure police services and not let the unions dictate department policies."

"Sir, I am sure you understand. The officers will continue to go around you to the city manager and council, despite our long-standing department order requiring officers to follow the chain of command."

"I hear you. Let's stay the course. We will talk later. Thank you, Captain."

Ty finished his day, went home, and thought about his conversation with the captains.

Metro PD was a three-legged stool, and two of the three legs were weak. The police union leg was fractured, the city council leg appeared fractured, and the city manager leg was becoming fractured. The stool was becoming unstable, and Ty needed some glue to hold it together. He remained focused on providing community-oriented policing.

Training is always a key to a solid organizational foundation and success. Ty attended a one-week police chief training retreat where the sessions covered topics like team building, police unions, and no-confidence voting by police unions against their chiefs. The first seminar instructor discussed the devasting power and impact of a no-confidence vote by the police unions against the police chief.

"Thank you, chiefs, for attending," the instructor, who was a retired police chief, began. "In discussing the no-confidence option, you all must understand this crucial issue. It is a powerful political weapon used by the union to get their way on department policies and issues. There are conditions in a city that promote an atmosphere of no-confidence voting by police unions and associations. The no-confidence vote by a police union against the chief is referred to as the nuclear option. Generally, this type of vote doesn't occur in cities where the officers are well paid, belong to an affluent community, and have a pleasant working environment.

"Be this as it may, the nuclear option is used against police chiefs. This is especially true if there are financial problems, a high crime rate, or a tumultuous political environment. However, for those of you who are chiefs in smaller cities, especially in rural communities, you run the highest risk."

"Let me get this right," Chief Charleston spoke up. "If I work in a quiet, low-crime, and affluent community, my officers will be fine. But if I work in a rural, high-crime, poor community with old police equipment, they may become discontent, form an alliance with the city manager or council, and attempt a coup through the use of a no-confidence vote?"

"Absolutely! It is now part of the additional challenges of being a police chief in America, especially in California. The irony is, the vote can be totally subjective, biased, malicious, and without merit—it doesn't matter. The impact will still be felt in the media, community, and city council meetings."

"So, if I hold officers accountable and discipline one of the clique members in the police union, they may subject me to a no-confidence vote?" Chief Robert asked.

"Again, yes!"

"Okay," Chief Charleston challenged. "Who runs the police department—the chief or the police union? How do we insulate ourselves from a corrupt or unethical police union?"

"Pick the right city to become chief!"

"Yeah. Where is our chief's crystal ball?"

"Okay, okay," the instructor conceded. "I know it is easier said than done because you just want your ticket punched as a police chief and move on! Listen, ladies and gentlemen, being a chief is a true balancing act. Technically, you have one boss, the city manager. But remember, the council ratifies every major statute in a municipality, whether it is the hiring of the police chief or other department head. Be cautious but not paranoid. I know you all understand transparency and accountability. Make it a daily habit and keep good notes about discussions and policy decisions with the city manager, council members, and police union—the three legs of the stool.

"If you have a strong, fair, and ethical city manager or council, the impact of a no-confidence vote is minimal and not a nuclear strike. Try not to worry about this political hatchet. As chief, you cannot be intimidated. Do the right thing all the time for the right reasons.

SYLVESTER STONE

"Work hard at not micromanaging your officers. This is difficult in a small agency. This is especially true if you see something procedurally wrong being performed by an officer. Document it and hand it to the captain or lieutenant to resolve. If it is a serious incident, improper use of force as an example, or a clear violation of law, leave it alone and report to the captain. Use your chain of command and let your sergeants and lieutenants handle minor violations."

Ty was approaching four years at Metro PD and was always getting tired of keeping his guard up. But he was surviving and making a difference—a long way from the racially hostile environment of his early days in policing.

Salary negotiations came around again, and the city manager asked Ty, "What do you hear about salary negotiations?"

"You know, the officers want higher pay and more days off, the usual rhetoric."

"Okay, keep me informed. I don't want them to start going to council members behind our backs."

"I completely understand. Thank you."

The police union had an ongoing battle with the chief, and many were disgruntled officers who believed they should run the police department yet weren't trained. Some tested for promotion but didn't have the academic education, experience, or training to be a sergeant or lieutenant. They were constantly complaining to the city manager about how the chief wouldn't let them arrest anyone and use whatever force they deemed necessary.

The city manager made it clear to them that the police chief, not the city manager or the council, was in charge of the police department. The city manager resigned, and a new city manager was hired. Ty believed the new CM's task was to get rid of him. Ty met and talked with the new city manager. Within a few weeks, the city manager called Ty into his office and told Ty complaints were being filed against him through the city council and city manager's office.

"Sir, this has been an ongoing battle with the union for years. Some of the police union members want to run the police department, kinda like the tail wagging the dog."

"I understand, Chief, but remember there is a new council in place, and they are taking the complaints seriously," the new city manager retorted. "As I am sure you know, there are two new council members, and they want to know why the complaints persist. So, they have ordered me to inquire and look into the allegations."

Meanwhile, several officers complained about being harassed directly by the chief for being late, writing poor police reports, and mistreating community members. Ty held them accountable for abuse of power, use of force, and other malfeasance against selected community members.

Some of the officers were simply not performing to standard. This back-and-forth tug-of-war continued with the city manager. Ty had thought the legs of the stool were somewhat repaired with the new city manager, but this wasn't true. The legs began to fracture even further.

Ty was accused of violating the due-process rights of some of the officers, who happened to be police union board of directors. Two of his officers were involved in an incident in Inner-City County, where policy violations and criminal charges were alleged. Ty followed procedure, and his IA sergeant began the investigation. The officers were placed on administrative leave with pay. Although this was the proper procedure, the officers filed grievances and complaints against Ty.

The city manager called Ty into his office. "Chief, I am initiating an investigation on the complaints filed by the officers."

"Fine, sir. I will cooperate."

The investigation lasted for about thirty days, and Ty remained on duty. The investigation concluded. Ty met with the city manager.

"Chief, the outside investigator completed his investigation and concluded that you didn't commit the violations of policy alleged by the police union. You are exonerated, Ty. Have a good day, and we will talk later."

While driving home, Ty thought, *All of this effort spent to get rid of me—we had many important tasks to perform, and this investigation brought a standstill to operational progress.*

The situation reminded him of the early days where he had been racially harassed. The current situation as police chief didn't appear to be racial in nature, only political. Although there were no Black officers in the department and only a few Hispanic officers, as a chief, he didn't hear any racial jokes or slurs from any of his officers, city managers, or the council. He suspected institutional racism but had no proof or evidence.

Ty and Chief Charleston went to lunch to discuss his situation.

"You know, Charleston, I'm not sure why this new city manager has joined with the city council and the union against me. I am just trying to respond to the public by holding the officers accountable."

"Ty, I heard the officers are conspiring because you have raised the standard of performance and changed their cushy working environment, and that includes some of your command staff. I have been in this county for more than thirty years, and generally, police chiefs can run their own department unless they have committed a crime, gross misconduct, or some sort of malfeasance. You haven't done any of these, and I am happy for you."

Ty shook his head in disgust. "I know I've ruffled some feathers, but I still don't get it. Why go after my career?"

"You realize being a police chief automatically places you in the line of fire, and in the political arena, everyone has an agenda, whether it's the police union, an unethical council member, or the city manager."

"Well, I'm going to fight back. This is wrong! The unethical, corruptive actions of the council and city manager should not be allowed to stand in twentieth-century America. I'm a military veteran who served this country, and I have rights too."

"Be careful," Chief Charleston warned. "Even though it's clear that the community, local police agencies, and the schools think very highly of you, they are not the council or city manager."

"Strange. The way I feel now is the same way I felt years ago when I received racial slurs and jokes from within my own police department. It stings big-time."

"You know, Ty, as I think about your situation, this may be another form of sophisticated racism against you. It is the one angle we have never discussed. After all, you are the only African American police chief in the county and in your city's history. In addition, you have no African Americans on the city council or your police department, and there's only one other Black city employee."

"I don't think race is the issue, but maybe I have turned a blind eye to everything. I've been there four years, and race never appeared to be the issue to me," Ty thought aloud. "I see the hostile atmosphere as simply political and corruptive in nature."

"Okay, not to disagree with you, but why else are you under constant fire for exercising routine, discretionary managerial decisions? What does the council or union have to gain by attacking you?"

"Good point, Charleston. I just didn't want to think that after all these years, the ugly monster of racial discrimination was alive and well in my life!"

"Ty, it's covert and institutionalized," Chief Charleston warned further. "It is not the in-your-face KKK racism—it's the subtle manner of the conduct against you that screams of institutional racism. Again, you're not being called the n-word to your face or being told racial jokes. Look at the unreasonableness of the harassment from the city manager and the city council against you. This constant assault is based solely on malcontent, unethical police officers."

"Well, I have much to think about. My eyes and mind are wide open!" Ty said. "Thank you. I really appreciate your words. Talk to you later, my friend."

Charleston and Ty left the restaurant.

How did I miss the signs of racial harassment in the hostile manner I was treated? Ty wondered as he was driving home. *I listened to the city manager, council members, and the police union. I focused on the mission of the police department, not the political turmoil.*

By avoiding the obvious, he had unwittingly misunderstood the officers, city council, and city manager. They were using the power of police unions to propagate a new form of discrimination—institutionalized racism.

As the weeks unfolded, the police union continued their assault against Chief Washington. They found ways to surreptitiously approach council members and the city manager. The city manager shared one of the complaints with Ty. "The police union says you require too much from the officers. You emphasize reports too much, and all the citizens want is a cop to listen to them. The police union go on to say your management style is too militaristic."

"Sir, my expectations are high and some of the union and. Some of the officers are lazy and use the excuse that many of the citizens don't speak English, and the officers don't speak Spanish and shouldn't be required to do so. Community policing means trying to communicate better with the community. Maybe I am unfair by providing training to learn Spanish and promote this as another tool for the officers."

"Chief, this sounds reasonable, and the investigation exonerated you, but I am still receiving complaints about your policies. They are also submitting the complaints to members of the city council even though the city policy requires employees to go through their chain of command before submitting formalized documents to the council. The police union chain of command is through the police department. As you know, they are not doing that but going to council through a back door."

"Thank you for talking to me about this sensitive and controversial matter. I will slow down and not hold the officers accountable and not push community policing so hard. They like busting heads, making arrests, and exerting the full measure of police power. That is not my philosophy. I will still not permit the use of excessive force, but I will relax my accountability process."

Ty braced to ride out this new political storm. He attended the regular city council meetings, and a council member took a verbal swing at him. The council member attempted to defame and discredit Ty by reading portions of the complaints in a public session, clearly a violation of privacy and due process. Ty didn't react or say anything in defense—he just listened.

"We cannot have a police chief like this," one council member said in an angry and direct manner. "He doesn't know how to treat his officers."

"Listen, there are always two sides to every story, and a city council meeting is not the right forum to hear these complaints!" another council member said next. "Remember, fellow council members, we hired the chief to run the police department, not the city manager or the council. I've read the complaints, and there are no allegations of criminal conduct, malfeasance, or any misconduct. Some of the officers have expressed their personal displeasure with the chief and his management style, not poor operations or misconduct. Let the chief run the department!"

There was loud applause from the audience. Ty was pleasantly surprised and pleased. This response illustrated support from the community. In fact, during the public comment portion of the council meeting, several citizens expressed displeasure regarding how Ty was treated by the council, city manager, and some of the officers.

"Council members, you hired the chief because of his training, education, and experience," a private citizen said. "Stop interfering and let him run the department. We in the public know why the officers are disgruntled with him—the chief refuses to let the officers run amok or mistreat the general public. He holds them accountable and requires them to perform their duties in accordance with the law and show compassionate understanding in dealing with us. His community-policing programs demonstrate to us, the residents of the city, just how much the chief cares about the community."

The audience cheered and applauded the comment.

A second citizen stood up. "Council members, do you not remember how crime was before the chief came? We had many thefts, assaults, and shootings. You all know perfectly well from the many presentations Chief Washington has made at previous council meetings how much crime has decreased in our city since his arrival four years ago."

A third citizen added his voice as well.

"Listen, council members. I have lived here for thirty years and watched police chiefs, council members, and city managers come and go. This police chief is in the community visiting the schools, going to the homes of residents, drinking coffee with them, and interacting with merchants at their places of business. No previous police chiefs have performed in this manner. Most importantly, the officers aren't mistreating citizens nearly as much as they did before the chief's arrival. Instead, I see the officers treating the public with civility, courtesy, and genuinely positive attitudes."

More loud applause from the audience rang through the chamber.

Several residents stood up and echoed similar sentiments and their observations about Chief Washington. This fiery council meeting ended, and for the moment, Ty was safe.

That night, he went home and called Chief Charleston and told him about the council meeting.

"Ty, I heard about the council meeting," Chief Charleston began. "Congrats, but it is only temporary. The writing is on the wall. For whatever reason, the city manager has convinced some of the council members to side with the police union against you."

"No way. That's ridiculous," Ty blurted, disgusted by this news. "There is no truth or merit to their complaints, and I believe the truth will prevail."

"Yes, I agree, but I am hearing the police union will not quit, and the legs on the stool are already fractured. This time it's not a hairline fracture but a severe one. If I were you, I'd prepare for retirement. You have enough time on the books. End this war before it ends you."

"You have a point, Charleston. I need to plan an exit strategy. But I will not go peacefully and submit to political injustice. You know, it's funny. Chief Ronald and I talked about this as well, and he agrees with me about fighting but also planning an exit strategy."

"I agree, but proceed with caution," Chief Charleston advised. "This is not going away, especially since you beat the council in an open session in front of the public. You've been there five years, and you've earned the privilege to retire with honor. Get the hell out!"

Ty sat in the living room and thought, his friends were right—policing was challenging, whether you were chief or a line-level patrol officer. Sometimes it was a rewarding career but not every time. Ty fought the good fight, and it was time to pull the pin and retire. He drove to the beach, walked on the pier, and began to think.

My childhood dream was to become a police officer and help society, Ty thought. *So, I go through years of racial degradation and harassment, racial jokes, and slurs from supervisors and colleagues. I stay the course and do everything I can to survive the racial assault year after year, police department after department, and getting fired. I become experienced and obtain graduate college degrees to survive and be the best cop I can. Too bad. I'm still subjected to overt and covert institutional racism. The army rebuilt my self-esteem, and I returned to policing. I became a chief of police. Wow, who would have ever believed this Black kid from the inner city would become one of the very few Black police chiefs in the country?*

Many years have passed, and now it is time for a new direction, Ty continued to think but now aloud. *I can teach college and go after a PhD. I really enjoy the college environment because my skin pigmentation is not a distraction, hindrance, or deterrent to success. My character, abilities, and energy are appreciated like they were in the military.*

Ty returned home and went to bed early, dreaming of retirement. He battled with the police union a few more months and, on his terms, announced his retirement from Metro PD. He was around long enough to see the city manager fired for misconduct, and the FBI began investigating the malfeasance of a certain city council member. After twenty-five years of police service, it was time to ride into the sunset. Metro PD was his last stand. There had been good and bad times, and he could investigate the mirror every morning and not be ashamed.

God had blessed him with a good career, children, and a host of good friends. It was said that when one door closed, another opened. Ty had been seeing doors open and close for nearly three decades, and his next chapter was retiring from police work. Ty met with some of his friends at the local Starbucks, a little coffee clutch, and talked about life after retirement. The chiefs talked about their careers, and Ty became excited at the thought of finishing his career. After several presentations by the MC's of the event, it was Ty's turn to speak.

When it was Ty's turn, he said, "Policing was a great journey and a quest to find equal opportunity as an African American. I went from being the n-word from fellow officers to finding political corruption and unethical police unions. It is on to my future and the second half of my life!"

His fellow police chiefs and former military friends arranged a retirement dinner for Chief Tyrone Washington. At the event, Ty was presented with numerous awards and commendations—not only from fellow police chiefs but also from community members and members of his police department. It was one of the most joyous moments in his life.

"I am honored and humbled," Chief Washington began. "I would like to personally thank each one of you for coming. I wish my mom were here to see how well her son did, the son she didn't want to be a cop but supported him, a son she didn't want to join the army but supported him. Thank you all for this outstanding event."

After a brief speech, which consisted of many thanks to everyone, Ty walked around and shook the hands of everyone in attendance. His brothers and daughters were in attendance for this most joyous occasion.

Life after policing, retirement, started with a great adventure for Ty. He became a college professor, teaching criminal justice, organizational behavior, and leadership management. Retirement was very beneficial to him. Ty's health improved substantially; his blood pressure and blood sugar normalized within six months.

His personal goal was to prepare courses to mentor other upcoming police executives about the dangers of political corruption and the lingering effects of racial discrimination. Ty thanked God through Jesus for his professional success. He wanted to give back to others, especially young people, through education, emphasizing how to develop successful life skills.

EPILOGUE

A Better Day for the USA

Ty's story is a vivid illustration of tenacity, diligence, and a never-give-up mindset. Finally, Ty began to understand why he had moved from agency to agency, even as a chief. The culture and environment of policing are not those of social understanding and acceptable behavior but rather those of tradition by the dominant members. The journey continues with ethnic disparity, social and political correctness, and position class distinction becoming clear—in other words, executive management versus line-level workers in the policing culture.

Ty's story is more common than many people may want to believe. His lifelong struggle with racism and his quest for social and professional equality was truly an American journey. Finding and identifying life mentors and coaches are essential to success. The importance of family values, education, and hard work cannot be emphasized enough. As Dr. Martin Luther King Jr. once said, "A threat to justice anywhere is a threat to justice everywhere."

Our great nation deserves nothing but the very best.

May 25, 2020, is a day that will live forever in the hearts and minds of many, since what happened to George Floyd and the many Black lives before him will now be memorialized in American history. The era of intense social change in America is coming. Police accountability and an emphasis on social justice, restoration of trust, and increased education on ethnic diversity topics will help unite our society. Ty's struggles continue; now is the time for action, not rhetoric.

This book will energize the racial justice conversation to the next level of resolution and bridge the racial divide in America.